Does that mean I think

The thought made Evette wince.
terribly irreverent, and she was glad she hadn't spoken the
words aloud for someone to hear.

She managed to still her trembling hands long enough to
open the car door and step back inside. After a long moment
she put the key back into the ignition. Coming tonight had
been a mistake.

The knock on the window nearly startled her out of her
seat. "You made it," Anthony said from the other side of the
window.

Evette opened the window cautiously. Now she was stuck.
Why hadn't she left sooner? "I can't stay."

Anthony gave her a puzzled look. "Why?"

"I–I forgot my Bible." A lame excuse. There were probably a hundred spare Bibles inside. She took a deep breath
and stepped out of the car.

Anthony chuckled and steered her gently toward the
church entrance. "Don't worry about it. I'm sure we can find
one for you."

Evette tried to hide her discomfort as she and Anthony
entered the classroom. She recognized many of the attendees
and noticed a few newcomers. Or maybe they weren't so
new. After all, she hadn't attended in years.

AISHA FORD resides with her parents and younger sister in Missouri. Through her writing, Aisha hopes to present a message of complete trust in Jesus Christ. "The best guide for living is to follow the biblical example of Jesus—the route by which we will reap the most lasting rewards," Aisha says. "Though none of us is perfect, God is the inventor of grace—and He is patient above and beyond what we can ask or imagine." Visit Aisha's website at http://www.aishaford.com

Books by Aisha Ford

HEARTSONG PRESENTS
HP362—Stacy's Wedding
HP405—The Wife Degree
HP461—Pride and Pumpernickel

Don't miss out on any of our super romances. Write to us at the following address for information on our newest releases and club membership.

Heartsong Presents Readers' Service
PO Box 721
Uhrichsville, OH 44683

Or visit www.heartsongpresents.com

Whole in One

Aisha Ford

Heartsong Presents

Dedicated to Mike and Aya Ford, my dad and sister. . .who patiently answered all of my golf-related questions. I love you both!

A note from the author:
I love to hear from my readers! You may correspond with me by writing:

Aisha Ford
Author Relations
PO Box 719
Uhrichsville, OH 44683

ISBN 1-58660-616-6

WHOLE IN ONE

All Scripture quotations, unless otherwise indicated, are taken from the HOLY BIBLE, NEW INTERNATIONAL VERSION®. NIV®. Copyright © 1973, 1978, 1984 by International Bible Society. Used by permission of Zondervan Publishing House. All rights reserved.

All of the characters and events in this book are fictitious. Any resemblance to actual persons, living or dead, or to actual events is purely coincidental.

Cover illustration © GettyOne.

PRINTED IN THE U.S.A.

one

Evette Howard brushed a stray curl away from her forehead and shoved it back into her ponytail. The sticky feeling from the heat and humidity was so bad that it almost took the fun out of practice. Almost.

She found it amazing that late April weather in St. Louis could get so warm. Still, given her family's line of business, she would take hot temperatures over cold any day of the week. The cooler the climate, the less likely people would be to go out and do anything related to golf.

Evette removed another ball from the bucket and positioned it on the tee. As she began her preshot routine, a soothing breeze rushed through, easing the intense heat for several moments.

As she prepared to hit the ball, her brother Craig's voice rang out over the intercom. "Evette, we need you inside, ASAP."

Taking a deep breath, Evette nodded and quickly hit the ball. She peeled off her glove, attached it to her bag, and replaced the driver. After counting her clubs to ensure she didn't leave one behind, Evette swung the bag over her shoulder and carried the bucket of balls inside the pro shop, where her dad and three brothers waited.

"Sorry to interrupt," said her dad. "Craig and Drew are supposed to go on lunch break, and Trevor and I have lessons to teach. We need you inside to watch the shop for a couple of hours."

"No problem. It's a little warm out there anyway. This air feels good."

"How'd you do?" asked Drew.

Evette shrugged. "Pretty well, I guess. Only got about halfway through, so I might hit more later. I wanted to put in a little time before I start lessons at three."

"Looks like my student is here," Trevor said, noticing that a car had just pulled up outside.

"I think I'll head out to the range and hit a few balls until Roger Stenson comes for his lesson," said her dad. "Are you ready to take over in here? Things shouldn't get too busy at this time of the day."

"I'll be fine. Just let me run to the ladies' room and freshen up." Evette headed off to splash a little cool water on her face, apply some perfume, and put on a touch of powder and lipstick. She didn't mind getting hot and sweaty out on the driving range, but she didn't want to mind the shop looking disheveled.

After her father and brothers left to teach their lessons and take lunch breaks, three customers entered the store in rapid succession. Two men wanted to try out different putters, and Evette pointed them in the right direction.

Then she spent time helping a woman on a mission find a birthday present for her husband. This proved to be a trying experience as the woman had no idea what he would like. After fifteen minutes of suggesting items ranging from golf balls to divot repair tools to a nice shirt, Evette convinced her to purchase a gift certificate in order to let her husband pick what he'd like.

She'd settled into her cove behind the desk to read over the latest industry magazines when the bell on the door jangled, announcing the entrance of another customer.

Evette instantly recognized him as Anthony Edwards, a member of the sizable Edwards clan who attended the same church she did. He had a twin brother named Albert, and both men were identically handsome. They shared the same height, muscular build, close-shaved haircuts, and skin the color of suntanned honey. The only reason Evette could tell them apart was because Anthony sported a small scar over his left eyebrow, a casualty of an accident during a game of touch football at a church outing a few years back.

As far as she knew, neither one of the brothers golfed. In the twelve years her family had operated the golf center, she couldn't recall either of them taking lessons or even stopping by the store to purchase golfing paraphernalia.

Anthony stood inside the doorway, apparently looking for something or someone.

Evette gave him a polite smile and asked if she could help him find something in particular. "You're Anthony Edwards, right? We go to the same church."

He nodded and moved a step closer. "And you're—Eve, right?"

"Evette," she corrected. "But when I was younger, everybody called me Eve."

"You used to be in the youth group, right? That's probably why I remembered you as Eve." He hesitated a moment, then said, "You know, it's been awhile since I've seen you at any of the activities or meetings."

Evette bit her lip, not sure what to say. She felt so uncomfortable whenever anyone asked why she was no longer involved in church activities. Going to Sunday morning service was about all the religion she could stand for a week. "I guess after I went away to college, I got out of the habit of going more than once a week."

Anthony looked thoughtful. "If you get the chance, you should come to Sunday school sometime or maybe to one of the singles' get-togethers. We have a regular group of almost twenty people."

Evette wrinkled her nose and gave a noncommittal shrug. Through occasional conversations with people from church, Evette gathered that Anthony was Mr. Church himself, always seeming to have his hand in some committee or other. From the youth basketball team to the choir and the church beautification committee, the man apparently loved being involved. "Maybe. We'll see."

An awkward moment passed between them, and Evette realized the look on her face suggested she had no plans of getting more involved. Anthony probably thought her a terrible heathen. She could almost see his wheels spinning, as he imagined some way to win her back into the fold. Weren't church people all the same?

He opened his mouth, and Evette braced herself for a sermon, feeling a twinge of frustration. Why couldn't people mind their own business? Wasn't it enough that she dragged herself out of bed early every Sunday morning and faithfully gave her tithes and offering every two weeks like clockwork? She always dressed appropriately, smiled at the pastor and his wife, and returned any hugs she received, especially from the elderly church mothers.

When Anthony spoke, he didn't mention church. "You're engaged to—Justin—Justin somebody, right?"

Evette swallowed hard. Even hearing his name still sometimes brought on a sick feeling in the pit of her stomach. "Justin Jenkins."

"That's right. I haven't seen him around, but he went out for the pro golfing tour, didn't he? How's he doing? You two set a date yet?"

Evette didn't know which of Anthony's rapid-fire questions to answer first. Ignoring the bad taste in her mouth, she cleared her throat and managed to put together a string of answers. "We're not engaged anymore. He did go out for the tour, and he's doing okay. Still on the semiprofessional circuit, trying to win enough money to get his membership card for the PGA—you know, the Professional Golfer's Association." Before Anthony had a chance to reply, Evette hurriedly changed the subject. "So—you must have come in here for a reason, and I'd hate to waste your time with chitchat. How can I help you?"

Anthony blinked, and Evette realized her transition to the next topic must have seemed abrupt. She felt a bit embarrassed, but she hadn't been in the mood to go into further detail.

Anthony moved on, seemingly giving the incident no further thought. "Actually I talked to Craig on Sunday about some golf lessons. He told me to come in and sign up."

Evette breathed a sigh of relief. This she could handle. "I didn't know you played golf."

"I don't. I can hit the ball a little, but not much more than that. I played with my sister's fiancé last week and totally embarrassed myself. This fall he wants to get all of his groomsmen out on the course the week of the wedding, and I need to have some skills by then."

Evette smiled, holding back the urge to laugh. It was no secret that Anthony excelled in whatever he played, from basketball, to volleyball, to football, and she could well imagine how he might have been irked to find he couldn't master the links in one afternoon. "I see. Well, Craig's on lunch break now, but if you want to leave your number, he'll be back in an hour or so, and I'll have him call you."

"How about I just come back later today?"

"That's fine. I'll tell him you came in."

"Thanks—I appreciate it." Anthony turned and headed toward the door then paused. "And don't forget—you said you'd think about coming to church more."

Evette pasted a smile on her face. The man did not give up. "I'll think about it."

The phone rang, ending Anthony's inquiries about her church attendance. He flashed a grin, then left without another word.

Evette decided to find a reason not to be in the store when Anthony returned.

❧

Anthony stared at the blank screen on his laptop. He needed to write the third installment of his weekly sports commentary for the newspaper, but he couldn't stop thinking about Evette.

At one time, several years ago, they'd been friends—or at least acquaintances. They were the same age and had been active in the church youth group in high school. They'd both gone to college here in St. Louis, but Evette's involvement at church had dropped off drastically over the past several years. She now put in an appearance only on Sundays.

Anthony wondered why she seemed to have such a distasteful attitude toward church. It made his heart twinge when he realized longtime acquaintances had slipped away from the church family without his noticing. Evette wasn't the first person he'd known to fade into the shadows. Nevertheless, he'd seen this scenario enough times to realize Evette most likely teetered on the brink of leaving and not ever looking back. Sure, she came faithfully once a week, but her habit was to slip in just before the service began and leave as soon as the benediction ended.

Her parents and brothers came every week as well, but none of them seemed to be involved in any further fellowship. Anthony didn't think being involved in church fellowship was mandatory, but he'd noted many who didn't get involved seemed much more likely to leave or attend more and more sporadically.

He'd been the same during his youth. In high school, going to church and being a part of the youth group had simply been a way to meet girls whom his parents would approve of his dating. And he supposed that if Evette hadn't been involved in such a serious relationship with Justin, he might have put more time into getting to know her.

In fact, if she hadn't had a boyfriend, he had no doubt he would have pursued her. She had a beautiful smile—when she smiled—and her complexion gave off an almost rosy glow. Her skin was the same color as his, maybe a shade lighter, and her hair fell to her shoulders in a thick mass of tiny gold and bronze ringlets.

For a woman she stood tall—at least five-ten, give or take an inch. With three brothers as her only siblings, she'd spent a lot of time outdoors, playing sports. While she had been on the skinny side back in high school, her figure was now healthy and athletic—not curvy and by no means willowy, but muscularly toned and strong.

Yes, if Evette and Justin hadn't been an item, Anthony knew he would have talked to her a lot more. But he hadn't, preferring to spend the bulk of his time with girls who were unattached and, therefore, had potential as girlfriends.

Anthony grimaced, remembering that phase of his life. He'd done his share of meeting and greeting and, ultimately, dating, keeping his social calendar full throughout high school and most of college. Yet, when he looked back at those years, he considered all of that mingling almost a waste of time.

At twenty-nine years old and striding down the corridor to thirty, he remained single, with no prospects in mind for a wife. Now that his baby sister, Dana, was engaged, his family turned their attention to the still-single twins: his brother, Albert, and him. The two of them had vowed to stand together and fight any attempts to make them panic at the thought of becoming permanent bachelors. It was a good plan—they were able to encourage each other if one of them felt a little impatient.

But Albert had been spending more and more time with Brienne Miller, a young woman who had recently joined the church. Anthony could already tell from the look in Albert's eye and the new bounce in his step that his brother found this girl pretty special.

So much for standing together. Anthony was on his own, with a bull's eye on his back that marked him as the last single person in his family.

Returning his attention to his computer, Anthony halfheartedly pecked out a few more sentences, but his thoughts were not on his work. He kept wondering what he might have done to keep Evette a part of the church family. If only he hadn't been so shallow about the manner in which he'd picked his friends. His mother would say there was no use in thinking about "what-ifs," and Anthony usually agreed. But he saw something in Evette's eyes to suggest that her outer demeanor of indifference didn't exactly line up with her true emotions.

With a sigh Anthony closed his word-processing program and shut down his computer. If his thoughts were correct, he wanted to do something about it.

two

"What do you mean, you can't take any more students?"

Craig gave Evette one of his I'm-the-big-brother looks. "I mean, I can't take any more students."

"But, but you—"

Craig put down the inventory sheet he was holding. "But what?"

"You told Anthony Edwards you would give him lessons."

"So? Why are you concerned about me teaching Anthony?"

Evette watched her brother's lips turn up at the corners. Oh, great. He had shifted to his teasing mode.

"Now." Craig folded the newspaper and laid it aside. "Are you sure you're telling me everything? How is it that my sister, who usually could care less about most people at church, has an unusual interest in the fact that some guy from there wants a golf lesson?"

Evette gave her brother a no-nonsense stare. "Don't tease me. You know good and well I don't care anything about him personally. But I do think it makes our business look bad with you telling him to come in for lessons, all the while knowing you can't take on another student."

"I never told him I would teach his lessons. Correct me if I'm wrong, but you, Dad, Trevor, Drew, and I all teach golf. We'll get your young man some lessons." Craig patted her on the head in a fatherly fashion, something he'd done for as long as she could remember.

Evette decided to ignore the "your young man" comment.

Craig *wanted* her to jump on it, and twenty-six years of being a little sister had taught her to leave certain comments alone. "Okay, then. Who?"

"Who, what?" Craig looked mildly amused.

"Who's going to teach him? Trevor works with the youth camps all summer, so he can't take regular students. And Dad and Drew have full student loads, like you."

"So you can teach him. You've got at least six or seven slots open for new students, don't you?"

Evette sat on the chair behind the register. "True. But, in case you've forgotten, we've tried this route before. I teach all of the women who want lessons because men don't want to learn golf from a woman."

Craig sighed deeply, a sign he had tired of this topic. "Then Anthony will be the first. Besides, you're a better golfer than Trevor and Dad, and your teacher skills are better than Drew's. Any student of yours should be honored to have such a good instructor."

Evette basked in the glow of this uncharacteristic compliment from the brother who didn't waste accolades on undeserving recipients. "Really? Do you think so?"

"I know so." Craig picked up the newspaper again, a sign he was finished with the conversation.

"You didn't mention yourself in that group."

Craig looked up from his paper. "What?"

"You mentioned everyone but yourself. So where do I stack up compared to you?"

Craig leaned back and let out a hearty laugh. "You've got to go a ways to beat me, Little Bit."

Evette groaned at the use of his childhood nickname for her. "Oh, please."

"Please what?" he asked, looking wide-eyed at her.

Evette glanced out of the front window and noticed that Anthony had returned, as promised. Smiling sweetly at Craig, she said, "Please tell Anthony why you're not going to be his teacher." She paused, then added, "I take it you explain things better than I do too."

Craig chuckled. "Whatever you say, Little Bit."

Evette picked up a box of raincoats. "Don't call me Little Bit in front of our customers. I'll be in the clothing section if you need me." Without glancing back she headed to the corner of the store where they displayed the golf attire. She was close enough to hear the conversation at the register but far enough away so she wouldn't have to contribute anything to it.

While she worked, Evette alternately listened to her brother and Anthony, then fumed about why she had to be the one to teach him. She had never, ever taught a man how to play golf. And she had a feeling that a guy as into sports as Anthony would not take kindly to a woman as his golf instructor.

She smoothed the wrinkles from a lightweight jacket and slipped it on a hanger.

"So I've signed you up to take lessons from Evette. I know you wanted to take from me, but we've had a big jump in our enrollment since I talked to you last week. I'm putting you in good hands. She's an excellent golfer and an even better teacher. If you're willing to pay attention and do what she says, you'll learn the game well."

Evette turned her head toward the two men and held her breath waiting for Anthony to answer.

"No problem. I'm ready." Anthony shook his head. "I'll tell you one thing. This game is a lot harder than I thought it would be."

Evette exhaled, her impression of Anthony growing more favorable by the moment. Any other time Craig had tried to assign her to a man, things hadn't gone well. One middle-aged gentleman had actually stomped his foot and started yelling for the manager when she stepped out on the range and informed him she was his teacher. Craig had come outside then and used his negotiation skills on the man to no avail. Eventually he ended up transferring one of Trevor's younger students to Evette's roster to appease the irritated customer. Even that hadn't worked out smoothly. The boy Evette inherited from Trevor was only thirteen years old and resented the fact that he had to learn golf from a "girl." Evette could still remember the way he said *girl* with such disdain.

"Evette," called Craig, "could you please come over here and schedule Anthony?"

Evette set the box down with a sigh. Craig knew full well her available class times were in the book, next to the time-table of classes and teachers. Calling her over to do it herself was his brotherly way of getting under her skin. Before she could point out that Craig could have done this on his own, Anthony spoke up.

"Hey, sorry to interrupt your work."

His grin disarmed her, and Evette returned the smile as she rummaged through the desk for a pen. "That's okay. I hate folding clothes anyway."

"I'll finish up the display," Craig said, heading off to the opposite end of the store.

Evette curiously watched her brother's retreating form. Funny how he was so eager to leave the scene. If she'd been dealing with Drew or Trevor, she might have suspected the matchmaking virus. Craig was different—the ever practical sibling who usually left such silliness to the younger ones.

Still, he did nothing without thinking the matter through from top to bottom and side to side. Though she wasn't sure why, he definitely seemed to be up to something.

But she didn't have time to think about it now since Anthony was waiting to settle his lesson time.

"Did Craig go over the rates yet?"

Anthony nodded. "Yeah. And we decided I should start with three classes a week."

Evette blinked. "Three?" Now she knew without a doubt Craig was up to something. The most they ever suggested for beginners was twice a week. More than two lessons would be too intense for someone simply trying to learn the game for recreational purposes.

Anthony leaned forward, craning his neck to get a look at the grid of open class times. "Do you have enough time for three?"

Evette tapped the pen against the desk, thinking. "No, that's not it. I just think three lessons per week might be too much to begin with. You don't want to get overwhelmed. I think once or twice would be better."

Anthony looked disappointed. "Are you sure? I mean, I really want to have this down by the time the wedding rolls around."

Evette couldn't hold back a laugh. "I can't promise you'll be a good golfer even if you take two classes a day every day until then. But if you want to come to the driving range on days you don't have a lesson, that might work well for you."

"Fine. Let's get this started. What days can I come?"

"I'll try to work around your schedule," Evette told him. "You're a sportswriter, right? So if you report on a game, you wouldn't be able to have class that evening."

Anthony frowned. "You're right. Does that mess things up?"

"No, not really. What we'll do is set your times at the begin-ning of the week to make sure you don't have a conflict."

"Fine with me. Can we start tomorrow?"

"Sure. How about five-thirty?"

"Good for me. An hour?"

"Correct." Evette marked Anthony down for the agreed-upon time.

"Good. I'll still have plenty of time to get to Bible study."

Bible study. Evette willed herself not to look up from the notebook.

"You know, if you don't have other plans, you might like to come along with me."

Evette blew out the breath she'd been holding. "I think I'll pass. I usually work on my own game after I'm finished teaching."

Anthony nodded. "Okay. See you tomorrow."

"Tomorrow," said Evette, her stomach already twisting with dread.

While she had been relieved to hear he didn't mind her as a teacher, she'd let her guard down. She'd been willing to believe his attitude suggested he might be interested in her.

What a joke. She now realized he must see her as some type of evangelism project. He hadn't even waited until his first class to invite her to a church function.

As soon as Anthony was out the door, Evette stalked over to Craig, who was nonchalantly folding polo shirts in the corner.

"You set things up?"

"Don't play innocent with me. Why did you tell him he needed three lessons a week?"

Evette put her hands on her hips and summoned her most effective glare.

"What's wrong with you? He's the one who wanted three lessons. I told him to try two, but he insisted on three." Craig shrugged. "He's a nice guy, you know, and he's still single."

Evette groaned loudly and held up her hands. "Don't you start with me. I don't need anyone. I'm fine, okay?"

An expression of guilt washed over Craig's face, and he stared at her for a long time. He folded a few more shirts then, ignoring Evette as she fumed.

"Fine, Evette. But what do you do besides work and practice golf? Do you think it would hurt you to spend a little more time with him? What's so horrible about going to a Bible study anyway?"

Evette blew out a sigh. Not only had he tried to set her up, he'd eavesdropped as well. "It's none of your business, Big Ears, so just be quiet."

"Hey, what's going on out here? We can hear Evette yelling in the back." Her dad emerged from the storeroom, with Drew right behind him.

Evette chewed the inside of her lip, feeling as if she were five years old again. Craig wouldn't tell on her, but he'd let his disapproval be known if she failed to be honest.

"I'm sorry. It was my fault. I got a little upset about something Craig did to me," Evette said pointedly. Her mom had laid down the no-tattletale law long ago, but there were ways to get around it without actually telling what the offender had done.

Her dad looked skeptical. "Look—I hope you two are acting like this only because there aren't any customers in here."

"Sorry, Dad," said Craig.

Her dad still looked unconvinced and cleared his throat. "It's been a slow night. I'll come out and watch the store, and Trevor and Drew will run the driving range. You've been here most of the day, so why don't you both take off early? Like now."

"Thanks, Dad," said Evette. Even though her dad had given them the adult equivalent of a time-out, she could already feel the stress of the day melting away.

On the way to their cars Evette attempted to make things right with Craig. "I didn't mean to explode just then." She gave him a sideways hug.

"I know you didn't. I shouldn't have gotten in your business like that. We'll both feel better in the morning."

"I hope so."

"We will." Craig hesitated then spoke what was on his mind. "Just try to relax a little, Evie. I know you're still hurting over this thing with Justin, but you have to—"

Evette shook her head, blinking back tears. "Please don't tell me to get over it or let it go. I'm hurt, and I have a right to be. How would you have felt if Lisa had canceled your wedding with no warning?"

Craig didn't answer but patted her on the shoulder. "I know. . .I know."

Evette pulled away, wiping her eyes with the back of her hand. "See you tomorrow."

"Drive carefully, okay?"

She nodded her head as she stepped into the car. She had a feeling her brother would take the long way to his house to follow her and make sure she made it home all right.

Evette buckled her seat belt, eager to be on her way. Today had not been the greatest of days, and she needed to unwind. She knew her mother would be willing to lend a sympathetic ear.

three

"Evette from church is going to be your golf teacher?" Albert asked. He and Anthony were sitting in the living room, watching television. As usual, Albert seemed to take delight in clicking the remote faster than Anthony's eyes could adjust to each image on the rapidly passing channels.

"Will you quit that?" Anthony pleaded.

Albert grinned. "Quit what?"

"You know what I'm talking about, Speedy Fingers. Now pick a channel and try to stay there for at least a minute."

"Fine." Albert switched to a sports channel and laid the remote on the coffee table.

"Now pass the popcorn and tell me more about Evette."

"There's not much to tell. You know her about as well as I do."

Albert popped several pieces into his mouth and chewed. "That's it? Nothing else?"

"Nothing else." Anthony reclaimed the bowl.

"You know, I hardly see her anymore. It's like she dropped out of sight when she graduated from high school. And isn't she engaged to that one guy—Justin—I can't remember his last name."

"She was, but not anymore."

Albert ate a few more kernels while he digested this information. "She's pretty," he said after awhile.

Anthony laughed. "What's that supposed to mean?"

"I don't know. You seem really excited about these classes.

21

Does the fact that she's single have anything to do with it?"

"No. I'm thinking of a way to try to get her involved in church things again. I kind of get the feeling she might be a little lonely."

"Hmm." Albert grabbed more popcorn.

"Hmm, what?"

"Hmm, I think you're approaching this the wrong way. If you're interested in her, don't lie to yourself or Evette about it. Just ask her out. If you play Mr. Holy, trying to bring Ms. Lonely to church to meet more people, it'll probably backfire."

"What makes you the expert? For weeks you haven't talked about anyone but Brienne, and now you want to give me a speech about my golf instructor."

"I know what I'm talking about. I made that mistake with Kelly Pierce. While I tried to think of a way to get to know her better, she and Bill Hodge decided they were soul mates. And I was the one who spent all that time inviting her to come to different events."

"I see your point." Anthony snatched the bowl away from Albert, who was devouring handfuls at record speed. "If I decide I feel differently about Evette, I'll be sure to speak up."

"Good." Albert stood up from the couch and stretched. "I'm going to bed."

"That sounds nice, but I still have a column to write." As Albert trudged off to his room, Anthony flipped his laptop open and forced himself to concentrate.

☙

"Okay, try again." Evette stood back and watched Anthony hit a few more shots. The first ball took flight to the right. The second went far to the left. The third ball bounced off the mat and ricocheted off the railing between the individual tee boxes. Evette ducked as the ball flew over her head and finally landed a few feet away. The past forty-five minutes hadn't been much different. Anthony was right. He was a terrible golfer.

He heaved a sigh and put the club down. "Sorry. I don't know what I'm doing wrong."

"Don't worry about it. If you were perfect, you wouldn't need lessons."

Anthony nodded his agreement and prepared to hit another ball. Evette grimaced, wondering how much longer she could watch him do this. Raising her hand, she said, "Hold on. I think you do need a change of pace. Why don't we head over to the putting green for the rest of the lesson?"

"You think I'm that bad, huh?"

Evette smiled tolerantly. "No, but you're getting more frustrated with every bad shot you hit." *That means all of them.*

"The more frustrated you are, the less you concentrate. To minimize the chances of someone getting hurt with an errant ball, I'm going to use my authority as your instructor and end this lesson with an exercise that doesn't involve an airborne ball."

Anthony followed her to the practice green, where she explained the basics of putting. To her relief, he did much better. He possessed a natural flair for reading greens, and Evette watched him sink ball after ball.

When the lesson ended, Anthony was more positive, but his face still held a look of disappointment. "It's too bad I can't hit the ball worth beans."

"Don't be so hard on yourself. There are lots of professionals who would love to putt like that."

Anthony shook his head at her compliment. "A lot of good that'll do me if I can't hit the ball straight. I'll be way over par before I even see the green."

"Some people hit the ball well off the tee but can't putt at all. Even though it might not look that way, the short game is really a big percentage of the entire strategy."

"I hope you're right." Anthony leaned on his putter and grinned. "Thanks for the lesson. I'll see you again Thursday."

"Five-thirty," Evette reminded him.

"Sure you don't want to come to Bible study with me tonight? Starts in an hour."

Evette felt her stomach tighten. "You know, I think I made myself clear yesterday. I'm not interested." As soon as she finished talking, Evette wished she hadn't sounded so harsh.

"Hey, I didn't mean to offend you. I just thought—" He didn't finish but picked up his clubs. "I'll see you Thursday."

After Anthony left, Evette went inside to freshen up. She was still upset that Anthony had invited her. She wished she could forget all about the discussion, but now she couldn't stop wondering if she should have agreed to go.

The fact that she didn't need his invitation to go irked her all the more. She was a member of the church as well and had a right to attend any of the functions without being invited.

I belong there as much as he does, but he's obviously asked me to come because he thinks I need spiritual guidance or something.

Evette strode into the pro shop.

"Your lesson go well?" asked Trevor.

"I guess. He'll be back on Thursday so maybe we'll have more progress on the driving range." Evette sat on one of the bar stools in the register area. Several customers came through, but not so many that the store was full.

"Where's Craig?"

"Out getting sandwiches for dinner," said Drew.

"And Dad?"

"Went home early since he didn't have to teach."

"Would you guys mind if I left early? Like now?"

Drew lifted his eyebrows. "I don't have a problem with it. You have to go somewhere?"

"Sort of." Evette grabbed her purse and keys. "Thanks. See you in the morning." She got into her car and, without even thinking about where she was headed, made her way to the church fifteen minutes later.

When she stepped out of the car, Evette realized she didn't have her Bible with her. Great. Anthony probably already thought the worst of her. Walking in without a Bible would only make him think he was right.

Evette stood with her hand on the car, debating her next move. The parking lot was filled with well over thirty cars so she supposed she might be able to sneak in unnoticed and leave as soon as things ended. That way Anthony would have no further reason to hold her nonattendance over her head.

Her other option would be to forget it and go back to work. At least she wouldn't have to worry about facing any uncomfortable questions about why she hadn't come in so long. Clearly, the latter would be easier.

Evette stared at the church door, remembering how much time she'd spent here in her youth. Getting out of the habit had been so easy. Missing a Bible study here, a Sunday school class there, and conveniently working at her summer job during singles' meetings. Not to mention all the time she'd spent with Justin.

Her commitment to attending church had fallen apart so slowly at first, like an old hand-knit scarf she used to have. At first it had been easy to tuck in a few loose threads here and there, but one day it became entangled on something in the washing machine and ended up looking more like a pile of yarn rather than anything wearable.

The same went for the time she'd injured her Achilles tendon playing soccer and had to quit the team. At first she'd kept up her fitness routines the best she could, but after awhile, looking at the time she'd lost from soccer, getting back in shape had seemed impossible. She'd already missed a big part of the season. So she quit working out.

But a month later Evette realized that not working out would only hurt her more the next season. And she still wanted to play with the volleyball team and run track. Unwilling to lose sight of her goal, she forced herself to resume her workouts. The first week had been the hardest, but she was able to get past that by focusing on the reason she was there—the love of the sport.

In all honesty the same reasoning should have applied to church. But she'd been away from this type of fellowship for much longer than a month—more like six years of months.

Why didn't I go back? Her soul was not in mortal danger—she'd asked Jesus into her heart when she was eight. After she died she knew she would live in heaven for eternity.

I try to obey the Bible. I give money to the offering. I put in a respectable amount of Sundays in church. I buy calendars from the annual fund-raiser.

Something about those actions felt dry and empty. Spending time at church didn't have the same appeal as the thrill of victory she experienced upon her return to soccer. She had resumed her workout routine because she missed it. Soccer, volleyball, track, golf—they were a part of her she couldn't bear to let go. She needed them.

But did she need church? Apparently not. Unlike sports she had no misgivings about staying away from church.

Does that mean I think I don't need God?

The thought made Evette wince. Something about that

seemed terribly irreverent, and she was glad she hadn't spoken the words aloud for someone to hear.

She managed to still her trembling hands long enough to open the car door and step back inside. After a long moment she put the key back into the ignition. Coming tonight had been a mistake.

The knock on the window nearly startled her out of her seat. "You made it," Anthony said from the other side of the window.

Evette opened the window cautiously. Now she was stuck. Why hadn't she left sooner? "I can't stay."

Anthony gave her a puzzled look. "Why?"

"I—I forgot my Bible." A lame excuse. There were probably a hundred spare Bibles inside. She took a deep breath and stepped out of the car.

Anthony chuckled and steered her gently toward the church entrance. "Don't worry about it. I'm sure we can find one for you."

Evette tried to hide her discomfort as she and Anthony entered the classroom. She recognized many of the attendees and noticed a few newcomers. Or maybe they weren't so new. After all, she hadn't attended in years.

The study leader, Tim Wilson, made sure a round of introductions took place for Evette's benefit, then began the lesson, mercifully shifting the attention away from Evette.

Tim and Anthony had located a Bible for her, and Evette kept up appearances by dutifully flipping to the appropriate chapters and keeping her eyes on the pages while the verses were read.

Other than that, she had trouble concentrating. The discussion was about showing God's love to those who didn't know about Him, and Evette wondered if Anthony had known about the topic in advance. She couldn't get past the suspicion that she was the guinea pig, the object lesson.

She half expected Anthony to get up and announce, "See—it worked on Evette. Two days ago she didn't want to come, but I kept praying, and she finally decided to come."

To her great relief he did no such thing. She felt defensive, though, by the time class ended. She couldn't ignore the curious stares from the other attendees. Some seemed surprised. Others seemed to give her the prodigal-has-returned look—an odd expression of pity and curiosity. She didn't need their sympathy.

I am just as saved as every one of you. Evette kept her head up and refused to feel intimidated.

She couldn't help imagining, though, what would happen if she jumped up and honestly spoke her mind. *I'm not your target! I come here every Sunday. Go help somebody else—you don't need to waste your energy on saving me!*

As soon as Tim prayed to close the meeting, Evette headed out the door, not bothering to wait for Anthony. She was still angry with him for dragging her here under these circumstances. She wanted to tell him exactly what she thought of his trick, but she didn't trust herself not to burst into tears. It didn't matter. She'd deal with it at his next lesson—if he had the nerve to show up.

As soon as she reached her car, Evette had to search in her purse for her keys. When she finally located them, they fell on the ground, just as Anthony burst out the door.

"Is everything okay?" His voice was the perfect mix of innocence and concern—obviously well practiced.

She held up her hand to stop him. "Don't go there. I thought you were a nice guy."

Ignoring her hand Anthony took a few steps closer. "What

are you talking about?"

She swallowed back the lump in her throat and blinked to keep her tears at bay. "This. You set me up." Putting her hands on her hips, she continued. "So what prize did you win for bringing me in?"

Anthony laughed. "Prize?"

Evette didn't see how he could keep up this confused act. "Yeah, prize. I know how these things go because I used to participate in them. Bring the most friends and get a gift certificate or something. Maybe a new Bible. You know, a gift in exchange for a poor, lost soul."

Anthony's face lit up with understanding. "Okay, Evette. Sometimes we do have things like that. But I promise you, that wasn't why I asked you to come."

"Then why did you ask me here?"

Emotions Evette couldn't read flickered across his face. Anthony opened and closed his mouth several times, and she knew he was trying to construct an answer.

"Don't bother." Evette opened the door and stepped into the car.

Anthony rushed over and begged her to roll the window down. Evette wanted to drive off and leave him standing there, looking as embarrassed as she felt, but she couldn't.

All right. She rolled the window down to the halfway point.

Anthony peered down at her, his fingertips resting on the window, as though that would prevent her from closing it before he finished explaining.

"I'm sorry you're feeling hurt. I honestly didn't know we were going to have that discussion tonight, and if I had known, I. . ." His voice trailed off.

Evette waited for Anthony to say he wouldn't have invited

her if he had known what the topic was, but he didn't. Instead he took a different approach.

"I'm sorry if you felt uncomfortable, but my intention wasn't to hurt you."

"You thought humiliation would be a better method?"

"No. I promise you. I just wanted you to come. I thought you might have fun."

Evette chewed the inside of her lip. She couldn't stay here all night, arguing over Anthony's true intentions. "Well, I didn't have fun."

She started the ignition and gave Anthony a pointed look. "Now will you get your fingers out of my window?"

Anthony stepped back, his shoulders drooping. Evette drove away without looking back, her emotions careening back and forth between disappointment and hurt.

four

"I told you."

"Do you have to say that?"

"I guess not, but it felt good."

Anthony kicked off his shoes and put his feet up on the coffee table.

Albert wrinkled his nose and gave Anthony's feet a shove. "Hey, we agreed. No feet on the table. What if we have company? Nobody wants to put a drink on a table that smells like feet."

Anthony scowled at his brother. "You could at least make an exception for stressful situations."

Albert was adamant. "Then eat some ice cream. But no feet on the table."

"Evette thinks I asked her to come to church so I could show her how much she needs to repent."

"Did you?"

"No. And yes. She kind of dropped out of the church population, and I think it would be good for her to come back."

"Maybe you should let her decide when she needs to do that."

"I guess you're right. But I didn't hurt her feelings on purpose tonight. It happened before I realized what was going on."

"So apologize and let it go. Obviously she's not ready."

Anthony couldn't let the matter drop. "I know she wants to be there. I can see it in her eyes."

Albert shook his head. "I think you're barking up the

wrong tree. And you sound like Mom or Aunt Florence with that see-it-in-the-eyes business. If Evette said she doesn't want to go, then what makes you think you know better than she does?"

Anthony couldn't explain what he felt. That same feeling—the feeling that he was about to witness another friend and believer drift away—was back, and this time his heart felt even heavier. "I can't make you understand what I feel, but I know she wants to. For some reason she can't—or won't."

Albert stared at him hard then finally said, "Do what you think you need to do, but I'd stay in prayer about it. And if you think you like her, then that'll confuse the lines even more. You have to make sure you're doing this because God wants you to and not because you think she's wife material."

Anthony sighed. Albert had a point, and he'd considered this since his confrontation with Evette after the meeting. He was attracted to her, and that did confuse things somewhat.

He laced his fingers together and leaned back, placing his hands over his eyes. Albert referred to this as his "praying position," and praying was exactly what he needed to do right now.

&

Evette awoke the next morning with a stomachache. And a headache. Along with a sore throat and stuffy nose.

Nothing unusual, considering she'd spent half the night crying.

Her dad left early for work and advised her to come in when she felt "up to it."

Her mother also got an early start to her day as a volunteer at the community center's literacy classes, so Evette was on her own.

After she showered and ate breakfast, Evette mulled over

the idea of going in to work. She didn't like the idea that she had special privileges, but she also didn't relish the idea of spending the entire day with her dad and brothers watching her like a hawk.

As she went over the pros and cons of whether or not to go to the shop, the doorbell rang.

The visitor turned out to be a florist deliveryman, bearing a small arrangement of colorful wild flowers.

"For Evette Howard," the man said, reading from a clipboard.

"Me?"

"Sign here, please, right next to the X," he said, handing her a pen and sheet of paper.

Evette signed hurriedly, anxious to see who had sent the bouquet. She hadn't received flowers since—well, not in a long time.

She shut the door and ripped open the envelope. The note was short and simple. *I'm sorry—Anthony.*

It wasn't long, eloquent prose or even a love note, but Evette felt tears come to her eyes. Maybe she had acted too presumptuously last night. Even through her anger, she'd had a hard time believing Anthony had invited her to make her feel badly.

Maybe I should call him and let him know I'm not upset anymore, she wondered. Or maybe not. After all he had a lesson tomorrow; she could tell him then.

❧

Later that afternoon Evette was ready to head out to the range for her four o'clock lesson when Anthony stopped by the pro shop.

"Did you get my note?" he asked.

Evette grinned at him. "Yes, and the flowers were beautiful."

"I'm glad you liked them."

Craig and Drew, who were standing at the register area with her, wandered off to a different part of the store, giving Evette and Anthony a little privacy.

Evette stared down at the desk and bent a corner of a sheet of paper, trying to formulate her thoughts into words. "I guess I should be the one to apologize. I shouldn't have lost my temper like that. Will you forgive me?"

"Definitely." Anthony cleared his throat. "And I guess I have a confession to make."

Evette studied him carefully. He'd already admitted he didn't want her to get hurt, so what could he possibly be about to admit?

"You see, I did want you to come to church, but part of the reason was because I wanted to see you again. Soon. Maybe I should ask you to forgive me too."

"Oh." Evette didn't know what else to say. The sentiment was both flattering and frightening. Considering the circumstances with Justin, she wasn't quite sure she felt confident enough to jump into another relationship.

Anthony must have sensed her reticence, because he backed away from the counter. "So is the lesson still on for tomorrow?"

Evette swallowed and forced herself to talk. "Yes. I'll see you then?"

"Five-thirty," Anthony said, heading toward the door.

As soon as he left, Evette exhaled and realized she'd been holding her breath. A million emotions washed over her at once.

Anthony's attraction wasn't one-sided, but she didn't know how to approach a relationship with him. Would he ultimately turn out similar to Justin, or was he truly different?

The question nagged at her for the rest of the day, and that evening she went home utterly exhausted.

She tried not to think about Justin or Anthony, but her resolve crumbled. Long after she went to bed, she still lay awake, wrestling with her feelings.

She could remember the last time she had spoken to Justin. He'd called on a Monday morning, just before she headed off to work.

"Sweetheart, it's me."

"Hi, Justin. I'm sorry about the tournament yesterday. I prayed for you, but maybe you'll do better at the next one."

"Yeah, I hope so." He didn't bother to hide the defeat in his voice.

Evette felt the tension growing over the phone, and she struggled to keep the mood light. "I'm just about to leave for work. Did you get your flight arranged? What time should I pick you up at the airport?"

Silence from his end of the line roared in her ears, and Evette knew something wasn't right. "Justin? Please don't tell me you're not coming home again this week?"

He cleared his throat. "Sweetheart—I don't know how to say this."

"Oh." Evette had her answer. He had decided to forgo coming home, yet again.

Another heavy sigh from his end. "Evette—you know how important golf is to me."

Evette nodded and tried to find her voice. Of course she knew how much golf meant to him. He had talent, and with more experience he could do well as a pro.

She felt the tiniest bit frustrated that he had insinuated she didn't know how much the game meant to him. Wasn't she his biggest fan? The one who had encouraged him to keep trying even when he didn't do well in a tournament?

"Sure I do. We both know." Evette licked her dry lips and

tried to keep her voice from cracking.

"I just think I need to spend more time going after this. I'm not getting a feel for things when I keep leaving and coming home for long stretches. The guys out here who make strides are the ones who stick with it and play more tournaments."

Evette knew then where he was taking the conversation, and she felt tears pool in her eyes. "So you're going to play full time?"

"Yeah. That's my plan—I hope you understand."

"I do—I understand. I mean, you'll be gone a lot when you make the tour so I guess I should get used to it. So—any estimate on when I'll get to see you again?" She tried to keep her voice light because she didn't want him to know how upset she felt.

When they first agreed he should play the preprofessional tour, Justin had committed to playing one or two tournaments a month, then working at her dad's range and pro shop the remaining weeks.

"I don't know yet," he finally answered.

Evette felt herself growing impatient with his nonverbal mood. Trying to talk to him when he got like this was like pulling teeth.

"Then when will you be home? Tell me what you're thinking. Dad's counting on you to work at least two weeks out of the month, and he'll want to know when you'll be home. And what about your students? It's difficult for them to be juggled between you one week and Craig the next. Plus, it's not fair to Craig. He already has enough students—"

"Evette. Don't stress over it. I might be home only one or two weeks this summer so it's obvious I can't teach anymore. I'll split my students between your brothers."

"But—"

"I'll call your dad and explain it to him myself. We'll work it out between the two of us."

Evette felt as if the wind had been knocked out of her. With those words she knew he had begun to cut her away from him. But she was determined to salvage this relationship. She hadn't given Justin the last eight years of her life for no reason.

"Look—I know how you feel about the tour, but don't you think it's a little inconvenient to spend so much time on the road right now? We're supposed to be planning the wedding and looking for a house. I thought we decided you wouldn't pour all of your time and money into this right now."

"No, Evette, that's what you decided, and I didn't argue because I didn't want to upset you. I'm so close I can almost taste this. I'm getting closer but making silly mistakes—losing by a few strokes. I need to keep my focus, and the only way I can do that is to play more successive weeks."

Evette counted to twenty to keep from losing her temper. Their wedding was set for December, and if Justin stayed on the tour for longer than four months, pulling off a wedding would be difficult at best. "So when will you be home? I guess I'll have to plan most of the wedding by myself."

"That's the other thing I wanted to discuss."

"The *other thing?* What on earth are you talking about?"

"Let's postpone the wedding, Evette. Please."

"Why?"

"Because I can't have it hanging over my head. I need to make the tour, and it's already July. If I'm going to make enough money to get my card, I need to be consistent over the next few months. If I'm close, but not close enough, I won't want to break my momentum for the wedding."

Evette was stunned, but she was determined to keep calm. "So the wedding is off for how long?"

"Indefinitely."

"I see."

"Evette, don't be angry with me."

"I'm trying not to, but it's hard. Twenty minutes ago I had a definite future, and now you've pulled the rug out from under my feet. What would you do if you were in my shoes? Honestly."

"I'd be upset. But this might be a good thing."

"A good thing? How is that?"

"I don't know. Think about it. We've been a couple since the eleventh grade. Eight years is a long time, and even though we're adults we've been connected to each other for so long. Maybe it's time we learned how to be independent of each other."

Evette didn't understand what he meant, but she tried to be understanding. "Maybe we should talk about this later. May I call you this evening?"

"I'll have to call you. I've got a flight to Arizona in an hour for this week's tournament."

Evette blinked. The deadline for entering the tournament had already passed. Obviously Justin had entered several days ago and had neglected to tell her until now. There was nothing more to say. He had broken their promise to be honest with each other, and that hurt more than anything else he'd said.

"I see," she said flatly. "Then we'll talk when you have time to pick up the phone."

"As soon as I get settled, we'll talk."

"All right. If I'm not home you can call the store."

"I'll do my best. But it might not be until tomorrow afternoon. I've got a bunch of other things to take care of since

I'm going to be on the road so much."

Even as they said their good-byes, Evette still held on to the hope that she could convince him not to postpone the wedding.

❧

Remembering that conversation made her cry. Ten months had passed, and the pain still existed as a dull ache she felt every day.

Things had only gone downhill from that point. He didn't call that day, or the next, but waited a full five days. That call had been even shorter, and most of the conversation centered around how he felt he would do in the tournament.

Evette had to watch the televised games to get a glimpse of him, and as his phone calls grew less frequent she hoped to see him in interviews just to hear his voice.

The ironic thing was that ever since then Justin's game had become more and more erratic. He'd struggled to keep his game consistent and hadn't won a single tournament. In fact, his best finish had been tied for tenth with six other people.

That September he at least had the decency to come home long enough to break up with her in person. "The pressure of having a relationship is too much for me to handle right now. I need to be free and not feel tied to any place or anyone right now."

Evette felt like yelling, "What relationship?" They talked once a week, at best, for no more than ten minutes, and he seemed more and more like a stranger.

Justin also announced he was moving to Texas to work with a coach he'd met. He'd already secured a job to teach at a golf academy during the off-season. "By the time the tour starts again, I'll be ready. I've learned how things go, and I know more about competing." Flashing his biggest smile, he said, "I'm on my way to the real deal, Evette."

He seemed so excited that Evette had to remind herself he had just dumped her. She had the feeling that their relationship had been over for months in his mind.

The last thing he said to her as they stood on her doorstep was, "Please be happy for me, Eve. You're the only one who really understands how much I want this."

Evette nodded and went inside as he walked away. She didn't need to watch him leave. Emotionally they had drifted apart long before then.

Some of her friends and relatives had speculated about whether or not he had another girlfriend, but Evette preferred not to pursue that angle. She'd already resigned herself to losing out to the game of golf, but she didn't think she could stand knowing whether or not another woman had been involved.

Now she felt vaguely relieved that the relationship was over. The pain and hurt were still there, but Justin had been right about one thing. She was learning how to be an independent person again.

Letting him make decisions and decide where they should go had been so easy. If he wanted to go out to dinner, they went. If he wanted to play golf, she followed along. Even when she was tired and wanted to stay home, she agreed to his suggestions to show him how much she loved him.

Now she sometimes reveled in the fact that she could plan her own evenings and weekends. No, she didn't want to be single forever, but she was enjoying this new season in her life.

Which was precisely the reason she needed to be cautious with Anthony.

five

"That's it—try it one more time."

Anthony inhaled deeply and took a close look at the green. The ball was near enough to the hole that he didn't need to apply a great deal of pressure to the putter. He swung the club gently, being careful to imitate the motion of a pendulum on a grandfather clock. The ball responded by rolling directly into the center of the cup.

Anthony glanced at Evette. "So? That was like twenty out of twenty-five. That's better than my last lesson."

"You definitely have a feel for putting. It takes some people ages to get it down, and others pick it up immediately. I'd put you in the second category."

Anthony laughed. "So am I ready for the pro tour yet?"

A strange look passed over Evette's face, but she seemed to recover from it quickly. "I think your short game skills will have to be 150 percent to make up for all the wayward drives you hit off the tee. You can't putt your way out of the rough, you know."

"Yeah." Anthony sighed heavily, remembering some of the more absurd shots he'd hit at the practice range. "I guess I need to spend more time working on my swing."

"Don't be discouraged." Evette replaced her clubs in her bag and headed back to the pro shop, rolling the bag behind her. "Everyone always has something about the game they want to improve. And maybe you're just thinking too hard about your swing." She stopped walking and tilted her head

41

to the side. "How would you feel if we took your next lesson to an actual golf course?"

"Yeah, right." Anthony shook his head. "No way I'm leaving the practice range until I can play."

A smirk tugged at the corners of Evette's mouth. "Do I hear a touch of egotism?"

Anthony lifted his eyebrows and smiled. "Hear whatever you want. I know this much—I'm not going out to let every other man see how bad I play. It'll take me forever to get the ball to the green, and whoever's in the group behind us will get impatient."

She shrugged, apparently not seeing his point. "So we'll schedule a time when the course is relatively clear, and if someone behind us gets antsy, we'll let them play through."

Anthony considered that for a moment. Her idea did make sense. And he would just have to pray nobody he knew saw him out there struggling to learn the game.

"Okay. But the course has to be clear."

"I'll do my best to make sure relatively few groups are out there, but no promises. I'm thinking about a weekday, maybe around ten in the morning. And we won't play one of the more popular courses. Something small and simple to get you started."

"Good. I can deal with that."

"And, of course, I'll be sure I remember to bring my CAUTION: GOLF LESSONS IN PROGRESS sign."

"What?" Anthony couldn't believe what he'd just heard. "A sign?"

"Yeah, I use it for all my students. It's about"—she gestured with her hands, indicating an expanse of about three feet by five feet—"yea big, and it has bright orange lettering. It's mounted on a pole, and I'll stick it in the ground so people will be more understanding. It's the same concept as the student-driver sign you see in the back of some cars."

"No. I'll play, but we are not using that sign." Anthony could envision the scenario. Not only would he run into probably a dozen people he knew, but they'd see him hacking away at the ball, not making any progress, with a bright orange sign and a woman teacher to boot.

"Why not? I'm getting the feeling you've embellished your golfing ability to your friends, and you don't want them to find out you're just learning."

Anthony held his hands up in defense. "Hey, what was I supposed to say? Ethan and some of the guys at work are forever bragging about the low score they shot and how they have some new gadget that's taken five shots off their game. And I'm a competitor by nature. Did you think I could admit I didn't know a five iron from a sand wedge?"

"Ahem." Evette cleared her throat. "Doesn't that fall under the category of—lying? Tsk, tsk, Mr. Bible Study."

Anthony sighed in frustration. It definitely stung to be reprimanded by Evette, especially after his zealous and disastrous attempt to get her to come back to church more often. She had taken his apology well, but he sensed she still felt a bit put off by the whole thing.

Had he been conversing with anyone else at this moment, he might have argued his point a little longer, but he knew it was probably best to confess right now. "Okay, I lied. And I have repented. And I will tell everyone I lied to that I messed up. But before I put my nongolfing skill on display for the world in general to see, I want a guarantee from you that you will leave that sign at home. Or else I won't go. I can confess my lie. I can deal with having a woman for a teacher. But the sign will be too much for me."

Evette widened her eyes. "And now the truth comes out. You don't like having a woman for a teacher."

Anthony felt as if he were falling deeper into a hole and wondered if he'd be able to dig his way out of it. He looked at Evette, hoping he could find a way to apologize yet again, then noticed something that put him at ease.

The solemn expression on her face couldn't mask the glint in her eye. She was teasing him.

The two of them burst out laughing at the same time. "I couldn't help giving you a hard time," she admitted. "You fell right into it, and the temptation was too hard to resist."

Anthony nodded, still chuckling. It was nice to see Evette return to her usual good humor—even if the change came at his expense. Her laugh was one of the most melodious he'd ever heard. He could sit and listen to the sound for hours on end, even years.

A fleeting memory of his conversation with Albert wiggled into the corners of his conscience. He had to watch himself now. Otherwise he'd look up and find he'd fallen in love with this woman and not even remember when or where it had happened. Be careful.

Anthony cleared his throat and swallowed the leftover laughter. "So about this sign—"

"For the record there is no sign." She smirked again. "But now I kind of wish I had one. You looked so mortified."

"I felt even worse. Boy, am I happy to hear you were kidding."

Evette reached up and patted him on the shoulder, and he caught a whiff of her floral perfume. "Come on," she said. "You didn't think I was that cruel? I wouldn't try to embarrass any of my students. My job is to help build confidence, not rip people to shreds."

Anthony struggled to think of a profound or meaningful

reply to her statement, but when no inspiration came he decided to let the moment pass in silence.

After they went inside the pro shop, Anthony said good-bye, and Evette promised to set up a tee time for one of the next week's lessons.

He stopped at the exit and ventured a final question. "I'll see you at church on Sunday?"

"I know you see me as a total heathen, Anthony, but I do go to church every Sunday. I think I'm as much of a Christian as you are, but I don't feel the need to be in that building every waking hour to prove it." The edge maneuvered its way back into her voice again, and Anthony wished he hadn't said anything at all.

Before he could speak, she apologized. "I was out of line. Yes, I'll be at church, and I'm looking forward to seeing you there."

Anthony wondered at her sudden change of tone, but he decided it would be a mistake to ask her and useless to spend too much time thinking about it. "Talk to you later, Evette." He waved and walked outside.

On his way to the car Anthony felt like whistling. Something was different about Evette, and that was an answer to his prayers.

෨

Evette set her alarm for Sunday morning a half hour earlier than usual. Anthony might have an infuriating way of pointing things out, but some things he said made sense.

Getting to church on time hadn't been one of his suggestions, but Evette figured the least she could do was show up on time, instead of slipping in after praise and worship and leaving before the altar call.

It wasn't as though she were pressed for time. Her Sunday

morning routine was just that—a routine, designed to keep her interaction with other churchgoers to a minimum. At first it had felt good to escape their prying questions and supposedly well-meaning comments. But now it made her feel plain old lonely. Out of the loop.

Evette had spent the past few days reflecting on the breakdown of communication between other churchgoers and her.

As she began her young adult years, many people had approached her with comments and suggestions about her relationship with Justin. Some of those statements were merely irritating while others were downright hurtful. She rebelled by sidestepping them as best she could. Statements like "We missed you last Sunday" or "Haven't seen you around much lately. Is everything okay?" or "Just because your boyfriend doesn't like church doesn't mean you shouldn't come" she answered with shrugs and noncommittal phrases.

Part of her knew they spoke the truth while the other part of her chafed at the fact that they couldn't keep their mouths shut and just pray for her.

Evette quit attending church altogether for awhile, using the excuse that the Christians were too nosy and hypocritical. Now she was beginning to see the immaturity in her line of reasoning. Although people had the tendency to say the wrong things at the wrong time, she couldn't blame that on the fact that they were Christians.

She'd had customers in the store say harsher things, and she hadn't even batted an eye. People who went to church were simply imperfect people, hoping to grow in their relationship with the Lord, who went to church to fellowship with others like them.

By sheer mathematics someone was bound to say the wrong thing now and then. Evette knew she wasn't perfect, and she had been wrong to hold them to a higher degree of perfection than she could attain. Some of them probably should have kept their observations about the beginning and demise of her relationship with Justin to themselves, but the root of their concern had been valid. She and Justin, although Christians, had slowly begun to drift away from the church.

Yes, she was prepared to mend her rift with her church family. Anthony's persistence upset her at first, but the mere fact that he had not lost patience with her after the Bible study impressed her.

After slipping into a buttercup yellow silk jacket and skirt, Evette spent fifteen minutes coaxing her curls up into an attractive style. She swept on a light dusting of powder and blush then finished with a natural tone of lipstick and mascara.

Giving herself a final glance in the mirror, Evette was pleased that Anthony would get to see her looking more feminine and refreshed than she did during his lessons.

She felt certain he would notice the difference, but at the same time she wondered if he would think she had gone out of her way to impress him. Although the two of them had barely begun a friendship, Evette couldn't ignore the growing attraction she had for Anthony. Was it wrong she wanted to put her best foot forward?

With a shrug she gathered her purse and went downstairs. Her parents were having breakfast and not yet dressed for church.

"Evette, honey, you look so nice and fresh in that yellow," her mother said.

"I've always thought that was a nice color on you," added her dad.

"Thanks, Mom and Dad," she said, feeling pleased that her extra effort had already been noticed.

"I made waffles for breakfast. Are you hungry?"

"Sounds delicious, Mom, but I have to get going, or I'll be late," Evette said.

Wearing a puzzled frown, her mother asked cautiously, "But where are you going?"

Evette tried to appear nonchalant. "I thought I'd go to Sunday school this morning." She shrugged. "I think Anthony said it still starts at nine-thirty."

"Anthony?" Her dad picked up on the name. "The one who signed up for golf lessons?"

"That's him."

Her dad nodded then turned to her mom. "Claude and Mavis Edwards's son."

"Oh, yes. One of the twins."

"Right," Evette said. "Now I need to leave, or I'll be late."

"Don't you want to take your Bible, Honey?" asked her mother.

"Great." Evette pressed her hand to her forehead. "Thanks for reminding me."

She put her purse aside, then kicked off her heels before she ran back upstairs to retrieve her Bible. After five minutes of searching, she located it under a pile of clothes. She vaguely remembered setting it there last week after church. Perhaps it was also a good time to start reading it on a regular basis again.

Evette ran back downstairs, hobbled into her shoes, grabbed her purse, and waved good-bye to her parents.

The streets were not too congested so she arrived at the church as the clock on her dashboard flashed nine-thirty. People were still arriving. She was relieved she wouldn't have to walk in by herself.

Evette parked her car. By the time she grabbed her things and locked the door, another car pulled alongside hers.

She looked over to find Anthony in the passenger's seat and his brother at the wheel. Anthony flashed her a grin, and Evette waited until he stepped out of the car before she headed over to say hello.

She might have been mistaken, but he seemed a bit more spruced up than usual. Instead of the polo shirt and slacks she often saw him wearing, he was dressed in a pinstripe suit and colorful necktie. Did he have somewhere special to go after the service, or was he dressed to impress as well?

Anthony spoke before she could give the matter any more thought. "You know, that yellow is pretty on you."

He noticed! Evette was so tickled that she couldn't hold back a smile. "You look nice yourself." Keeping the mood light, she said, "I bet you're surprised to see me here so early."

He seemed to consider her statement a few seconds. "Actually I am. But I promised myself I wouldn't ask any inane questions and make you feel uncomfortable."

Albert spoke up. "That means he wants to know why you came, but he won't ask. If any explanation is given, you'll have to give it yourself."

Anthony playfully elbowed his twin. "Will you let me talk for myself? Last I checked, my tongue still worked."

Albert burst out laughing and shook his head. He draped his arms over Anthony's shoulder. "Hey, I'm just trying to be a good big brother."

Anthony wriggled away and countered with, "Three minutes does not constitute a big brother. In fact, three minutes barely gives you the right to claim you're older than I am."

Anthony stopped walking and stared at the direction of the church doorway. "Hmm," he said, a mysterious ring to his voice.

"Hmm, what?" said Albert, still laughing.

"Hmm, I think I saw Brienne laughing and talking to Ray Jenkins."

"Really?" Albert glanced toward the door and quickened his pace. Then he stopped and turned back. "Hey, Evette, it's nice seeing you again. Excuse me while I run in here and prove my little brother needs some serious glasses."

"Glasses?" Anthony countered.

"Yeah, 'cause I think you're seeing things."

"Whatever. I guess your brain didn't convince your feet, because you're still running inside, aren't you?"

Albert shook his head but moved even faster.

Evette giggled. "Who's Brienne?"

"The woman my brother's falling in love with."

"Did you really see her with another guy?"

Anthony wiggled his eyebrows. "Actually I did. But he doesn't have to worry. She likes Albert as much as he likes her."

"You are so mean. You got him all worried for no reason," she said, smiling.

"I wouldn't say 'for no reason.' I got him out of my hair before he had the chance to embarrass me."

"I know all about that," Evette agreed. "I have three older brothers, remember?"

"So you definitely know what it's like."

They were a few steps from the entrance when Evette said, "I'm curious—what exactly did you think Albert would say to embarrass you?"

"And I'm curious about why you decided, out of the blue, to come to Sunday school," he answered. "Do you feel like explaining?"

"Um, not yet." Evette wanted to tell him about her tentative change of heart, but she wanted to be certain she could keep her resolve before she went into great detail.

"And I can't tell you why Albert was teasing me. At least, um, not yet," he said, mimicking her.

The first step inside the classroom proved to be the hardest. The curious stares were back and even more weighted with unspoken questions than last Wednesday.

Evette hesitated for a millisecond, but when Anthony took her hand in his and kept walking, she had no choice but to follow.

The class seemed to drag on for the first few minutes until the teacher started tossing out Scripture references to look up and take notes on. Evette soon forgot her discomfort and immersed herself in the lesson.

After the class dismissed, several people came over and said hello and told her they were happy to see her again.

Evette tried not to view their comments in a negative light and took them at face value—as genuine happiness to see her again.

During the service she sat with her parents, and afterward several more old acquaintances stopped to say hello. Most of them invited her to come back for Wednesday Bible study and prayer, but Evette decided not to commit until she had given the idea more thought. For the time being she felt uncomfortable taking anything more than baby steps—like coming to Sunday school this morning.

After several minutes of greeting and hugging people, Evette realized her parents had already left. She worked her way through the crowd, heading for the nearest exit, and had just stepped outside when Anthony called her name.

Evette turned and waited for him to come over.

"Some of us are going to lunch, and I wondered if you wanted to come."

Evette rubbed her temple. As much as she wanted to join him and his friends, the earlier start to the day and the anxiety of getting reacclimated had taken its toll on her. Although it was only half past noon, she felt drained. The idea of a large crowd at a noisy restaurant gave her a headache. "I don't know—"

Anthony seemed to sense her discomfort. "Come on— you'll have fun. It'll be just you, Albert, Brienne, and me. If you don't come, I'll be the third wheel with those two."

Evette decided a group of four was much less intimidating so she agreed. "Should I drive?"

He shook his head. "No, we'll all take Albert's SUV, and afterward we'll bring you ladies back to the church to pick up your cars."

six

"Fore!" Evette shaded her eyes with her hands and tried to follow the path of yet another errant shot from Anthony.

"You know, there's no one else out here, so you don't have to yell. It's not like either one of us is surprised I messed up. Again." Anthony sighed and rubbed his hand over his head, wiping away beads of sweat.

"Yes, I do. It's part of the rules. You never know when someone might have stepped out on the course." Evette sighed as they trudged forward to locate where the ball had landed.

Anthony looked as frustrated as she felt. He still had seven holes to play, but Evette wished they could quit now. The June heat, combined with humidity, made her wish desperately that she could be swimming instead of out on a golf course.

Anthony stopped, pulled a towel from his bag and mopped his face with it.

Evette kept walking, intent on finding the ball. When Anthony caught up, she pointed to it and waited for him to take another shot.

With any other student she might have called out a few pointers as he prepared to swing, but she had given that up three holes earlier. Anthony claimed her incessant tips were making him nervous so she took the hint and said nothing more. But she felt a bit irritated with him at the moment. She was the teacher, and she could see at least ten mistakes he made each time he played a shot. If anything, he was worse since the ninth hole.

As Anthony moved through a rather sloppy preshot routine, Evette closed her eyes, unable to watch. After she heard the sound of the club head smack the ball, she waited for him to groan or complain.

But he didn't. Instead he let out an excited yell. "Oh, yeah!"

"What happened?" Evette opened her eyes and moved next to him.

"I'm on the green!"

"You are? From here?" Evette was happy for him, but she had a feeling he was mistaken. It would be difficult for even the most seasoned golfer to play a shot from this spot to the green. "Why don't we go make sure?" she suggested.

"Ha! You don't believe me, but it's there. Trust me." Anthony hurried ahead, apparently having caught his second wind. Evette did her best to keep up, but the heat made her feel like a wilted piece of lettuce.

Sure enough, Anthony was correct. Not only had he made it to the green, but the ball was less than a foot from the cup. He made the putt with no problem.

He leaned against his putter, looking so pleased with himself that Evette decided not to mention he had still shot an eight on this hole.

Besides, she was counting down the minutes until this round ended. She planned to go home and take a long, cool shower, then relax on the couch with a pitcher of iced tea.

Anthony looked thoughtful. "You know what?"

"I'm too tired to guess," she admitted.

"I think I'd like to end on a positive note. Let's call it a day. How about we stop for ice cream on the way back to the shop? My treat?"

Evette grimaced. "Honestly, I'm not even going to work the rest of the day. You're my only student, and my brothers have the store covered. I'd love to have ice cream with you, but not like this. I'm pouring sweat."

He nodded. "Same here. And I have a column to finish."

"You could come over later this evening," she suggested. "I mean, if you're not too busy."

He seemed to consider this then agreed. "Okay. Sounds good to me. Around eight?"

"Excellent."

After the short ride to the shop Evette didn't even go inside. If one of her brothers saw her, no doubt they'd ask her to stay and help with something. She was not one to dodge her job, but she was too worn out to do anything right now.

After a long, refreshing shower, she helped her mother cook dinner. Her mother seemed happy to learn that Anthony would be over later and kept asking why Evette hadn't invited him to dinner as well.

"Mom, it's okay. We can do that another day. Besides, he has a column to write. I know he'd come if I asked, but then he might be in a time crunch with his assignment."

"You know he'd come? It's getting that serious, is it?"

Evette laughed. "Okay, not that serious, but we do enjoy spending time together. Even when we're tired and annoyed, like today out on the course."

Her mother sat down at the kitchen table and motioned for Evette to join her. She reluctantly followed, but her mother's questions and willingness to listen put her at ease. Before she knew it, Evette found herself pouring out the details of her afternoon with Anthony.

࿇

Anthony arrived at Evette's house at eight o'clock on the dot. He hadn't been sure what kind of ice cream her family liked, so he'd brought three flavors—chocolate, vanilla, and a la mode. The third was his favorite—vanilla ice cream with real apple pie mixed in.

After Anthony was introduced to Evette's parents, they all gathered around the dining room table to have dessert.

"I told Evette she should have asked you to dinner," Mrs. Howard said. "Maybe you can join us next Sunday after church," she suggested.

Anthony agreed to come and chatted with Evette and her dad while her mother dished up the ice cream. Just as they began to eat, the doorbell rang. "I'll get it," said Mrs. Howard.

Evette and her dad were discussing a new floor display at the shop. Anthony was listening, but he could hear her mother conversing with someone at the door.

"Trevor! What are you doing here?"

"I wanted to talk to Dad. Is he here?"

"Well, yes, but Evette has company. Can it wait until tomorrow?"

"Actually, it's kind of important."

By this time Evette and her dad had stopped talking and were listening to the conversation at the front door. "Well, don't just stand there," her dad called. "Trevor, come in here and say what you have to say. Your mother's ice cream is melting."

"Ice cream? Now that sounds good."

Evette shook her head. "Mom, make him go home, please. All he ever wants to talk about is the store."

Anthony chuckled. Trevor was only a year older than Evette, and she had told him many stories about their close friendship and rivalry. Anthony leaned toward her. "It's okay," he whispered.

He tried to stay positive for Evette's sake since he knew she had hoped for a quiet evening. Apparently the evening wouldn't be as quiet as she had wanted, but Anthony didn't mind. He came from a large family and had seen many of his siblings' dates and parties similarly invaded—and many times he had been one of the intruding offenders.

Trevor strode through the hallway toward the dining room, still talking. "As a matter of fact, I have someone out in the car who wants to talk to Dad, so I can't stay long. Evette, I know you won't like it, but I think this'll be great for business." He stopped short when he entered the dining room and saw Anthony.

Evette stood up. "Okay, spill it. What won't I like?"

Trevor blinked slowly, seemingly deep in thought. "Well, maybe you won't mind, since you have your new boyfriend here and all—"

Evette flushed a deep pink. "Trevor, he's not my boyfriend. We're just good friends. And what does that have to do with whether or not I'll like what you have to say?"

Trevor grinned. "Oh, yeah? This looks kind of serious to me. It's a Tuesday night, Mom's all dressed up, Dad's not watching baseball, and you're sitting around the dining room table eating ice cream out of the fancy bowls." Trevor crossed his arms over his chest, looking amused by his analysis of the situation.

"Dad, will you tell him to go home?" she pleaded.

"Trevor, go home. But first tell me this important news about the store."

Trevor glanced at Evette, who gave him a withering stare. "You know, maybe this can wait until tomorrow."

"After all this fuss, tell me now," his dad commanded.

Trevor stood his ground. "Trust me, Dad. It will have to wait until later. Now is not a good time."

Evette's mother sighed. "Honey, was it worth all of that fuss? Why didn't you let it drop earlier?"

He shrugged. "I guess I got carried away with—oh, man! I gotta get back to the car. He—I mean, my friend is going to wonder what happened to me."

"What friend?" his dad asked.

"An old family friend who wants to talk to you about the store. But not now, Dad. I'm serious."

"Trevor, you are not making any sense," Evette said. "First you just had to talk to Dad, but now the big news isn't so important. What's up that you don't want me to know about?"

He held up his hands in defense. "Nothing. Sort of."

Before he could say more, the front door creaked open, and another voice called out. "Hey, Trevor? Mr. and Mrs. Howard? Is everything okay in here?"

Evette gasped and sat down in her chair.

"Justin?" her mother said. "Is that you?"

Her father stood up. "Why did you bring him here? Why not to the store in the morning?" He glanced back at Evette then gave Trevor a stern look.

"Dad, I didn't know she had—company. He called me an hour ago and wanted to know if I thought you'd give him his old job back. I just suggested we should come over and ask. . . ." His voice trailed off as Justin appeared in the doorway.

"Hi, Mr. and Mrs. Howard—Evette—and—" He cast a puzzled glance toward Anthony.

"Anthony Edwards." Anthony stood and extended his hand. "I think we've met a few times."

Justin nodded slowly. "I think I do remember your face."

Anthony felt the tension rising moment by moment. He knew Justin and Evette had broken their engagement, but from the reactions of Evette and her parents he had the feeling it hadn't been a mutual agreement.

Evette stared at the curtains while Justin focused on the

wall. Neither one seemed willing to make eye contact with the other, and everyone else in the room remained silent, probably trying to think of something to say.

Trevor spoke first. "We came at a bad time, Justin. You'll have to talk to Dad tomorrow."

"Oh, I'm sorry if we interrupted—something." He glanced at Anthony. "I was a little impatient and talked Trevor into bringing me over tonight."

"I'd actually like to discuss this now." Mr. Howard stood, motioning for Justin and Trevor to step out of the room. "You go ahead and start dessert without me," he said to Evette's mother after the other two had left. "I'll handle this in my office."

Evette sighed quietly. "What are you going to do?"

Her dad shrugged. "I guess I'm going to sort this out and find out why he's back and needs a job."

"You aren't going to hire him, are you?" This came from Evette's mother, her brow creased.

"Well—obviously I won't take him back if the other employees at the store have objections."

"You don't have to worry about me, Dad." The steadiness of Evette's voice didn't match the distressed look in her eyes. "If he needs a job and Craig and Drew want him back, then I'm okay. Obviously Trevor agrees, and I know you've been wanting to cut back your hours."

"Are you sure?"

"Not really. I don't feel good about him being around again, but I can work around his hours, and—things should work out fine."

Anthony felt increasingly uncomfortable. He'd accidentally been cast into the midst of a very personal family situation, and now he wanted nothing more than to get out. Fast.

Part of him wanted to stay and comfort Evette, who was obviously hurt, and another part of him wondered why her father and brothers seemed so willing to welcome this scoundrel who was responsible for her emotional damage.

Evette's mother started clearing away the dessert dishes, apparently having forgotten that the ice cream hadn't been eaten.

Anthony cleared his throat softly, and Evette jumped a little in her chair, as if she suddenly remembered he was still there. She leaned across the table and shook her head. "I'm sorry about this."

"It's not your fault; you don't need to apologize." What else could he say? Should he leave now or stay and pretend nothing had happened?

His thoughts returned to Justin, and he felt himself growing angry. He wanted some answers. Frowning, he spoke. "I don't know all the history here, so maybe I shouldn't say anything—"

"You're right," Evette cut in. "You shouldn't say anything. It's a long and confusing story. The gist of it is this: Justin and I were engaged, and he called off our wedding in a very tacky way. But before we dated, he was Drew's good friend, and he worked at our store for years. He spent so much time with our family that he seemed like one of us, and by the time we started dating, that just tightened the bond we had with him. As much as he hurt us, we are happy to see him— to my dad I think it's like having one of his own kids return. What can we do? Send him packing? Even you have to admit it wouldn't be very Christlike."

Anthony didn't know how to digest this piece of information. He certainly didn't want to try to determine how this would affect his friendship with Evette or her newfound desire to deepen her relationship with the Lord and with the people at church.

If anything, he remembered that in the past her time spent with Justin had kept her away from church, and he found it ironic that just as she'd decided to make this change, the situation appeared ready to repeat itself.

After Evette recovered from her initial shock of seeing Justin, he had the impression she was glad to have him back. Was she planning to rekindle their relationship? Did Justin have similar ideas? Anthony's stomach twisted painfully. He needed to think of a way to leave quickly, without offending her.

Evette rubbed her forehead. "I'm getting a terrible headache. Would you take a rain check for tonight?"

"Sure." Anthony stood up and followed Evette as she led the way to the front door. "I may need to cancel my Friday lesson. I have to cover the Cardinals' game."

I sound as if I'm trying to dodge her, he admitted to himself, feeling uncomfortable. *And maybe I am. Having her ex-fiancé here puts me in a strange position, and I'm sure she'd understand how I feel.*

Anthony cleared his throat. "I found out about Friday just before I came over," he added. In fact he had planned to ask Evette to come along. Now that didn't seem like such a good idea.

Evette opened the front door and smiled. "We can reschedule the lesson. When do you have some free time?"

"I—don't know. Baseball's in full swing now, and my editor has the entire department working overtime. I may even have to attend a few out-of-town games."

Evette's smile faded, making him feel even worse. The last thing he wanted to do was hurt her feelings or make her upset with him, but he needed some time to think about what had just occurred. He wanted to protect her from the hurt Justin had caused, but he also wanted to run away.

Anthony stepped outside the threshold of the door and stood face-to-face with Evette. There must be something he could say to end the evening on a light note.

"Well, thanks for coming," Evette said. "I wish. . ." Her voice trailed off, and she looked down at the ground.

Go home now, he told himself, but his feet refused to move. Even as he drew Evette into a hug, Anthony had second thoughts about the action. At first Evette seemed frozen, but after a moment she returned the embrace. Seconds later he pulled away, pausing as their faces were inches apart. Evette closed her eyes and leaned a fraction closer while he did the same. A myriad of emotions swirled in his heart, but he couldn't be sure love was one of them.

Do I love her, or do I only want to win her away from Justin? The echo of that thought hammered in his brain and held him back from kissing her. Anthony smelled the perfume he loved and felt her breath on his face, but he couldn't, or wouldn't, move a muscle toward her.

He took a step back.

Evette blinked and moved away as well.

"I'll be praying for you," Anthony said then turned and hurried down the stairs as fast as his feet could take him.

He reached his car and fumbled with the keys, wondering what in the world Evette would think of him now. "I'll be praying for you?" he repeated in a whisper. "What kind of good night is that?"

❧

He's running away. And literally at that moment he was running. *I'm not surprised.* Evette watched through the front window as Anthony dashed to his car and sped away.

With a sigh she steeled herself to face the reality of what had happened. Dad, Justin, and Trevor were still in conference in the den, the door shut tight. Mom was in the kitchen, clanging dishes around and running water.

Evette decided to elude all worried glances and questions for the rest of the evening and go to bed early. Trudging up the stairs, she recalled Anthony's last words: "I'll be praying for you."

Not very romantic, that was for sure. And what was the deal with the kiss-that-didn't-quite-happen?

Maybe I have something stuck in my teeth. On the way to her room Evette took a detour to the bathroom and did a quick mouth check. Fresh breath, nothing green stuck anywhere. *So why did he run?*

In her room she put on her pajamas, turned off the lights, and did her best to fall asleep.

After several minutes it became apparent that Sleep had forsaken her and left his enemy, Questions, behind to keep her awake.

There had to be something behind the sudden return of Justin. Had he given up on the golf dream? Or was he truly repentant? He had to be sorry. Why else would he come *here* looking for a job? Even if he didn't play at the pro level, he was skilled enough to teach at any other academy.

And what about Anthony? No sooner had they taken tentative steps to a relationship than things became confused. At first he seemed puzzled, then upset. By the end of the evening he was obviously making excuses about why he couldn't reschedule his lesson. A baseball game—how convenient. Then there was the business with the kiss—or nonkiss.

Did he think she was being too forward? Something had

made him stop abruptly. Then all he could manage to say was he would pray for her. The old suspicion that he had begun the relationship only to evangelize her returned.

Maybe he had never seen her as more than a friend. And now that she had an interest in being more involved in church, he was satisfied and ready to move on to his next project. The hug had been a mistake, a miscalculation on his part. Anthony's heart held no romantic emotions for her. He had proved this by his not-so-subtle attempt to steer the conversation to prayer.

Now that her analysis was complete, Evette felt relieved. At least Anthony had the decency to back out before she fell in love with him. As much as it hurt to admit she was disappointed, she could count him as a true gentleman, unlike Justin. Despite her attempts Evette couldn't convince herself that Justin had made any significant changes.

seven

"In spite of how you feel, I think you did the right thing. About the kiss—or the nonkiss."

"Easy for you to say. You have a girlfriend." Anthony dunked a sponge into the bucket of soapy water and wrung it out. On a beautiful Saturday afternoon he had nothing more exciting to do than wash his car. This was pretty pathetic. Heaving a deep sigh, he concentrated on cleaning the car as well as he could.

"True. But I spent a lot of time thinking and praying before I asked Brienne to be in an exclusive relationship—and relationships are not about kissing. There should be some serious commitment before you jump into physical contact like that. For example—"

Anthony hated to be a spoilsport, but he didn't think he could stand to listen to Albert waxing poetic once again about his wonderful girlfriend. All he could think about was Evette and how much he missed her.

"Hey!" Albert yelled. "I get the feeling you're ignoring me."

Anthony looked at his brother. "What now? Please don't tell me the story about when you sent the roses to her at work and all of her friends gushed about how sweet you were. I don't think I can stomach it today."

"I just wanted a clean sponge." Albert waited, his hand extended.

Anthony handed his brother the sponge and resumed working.

"You may want to call your car insurance guy." Albert stood

with his arms crossed, looking close to laughter.

"Why?" Anthony gave the car a once-over. "It looks okay to me."

"I think you're going to need a new paint job."

"You can't be serious."

"It's that one spot there that looks a little faded," Albert said, pointing.

Anthony leaned in to examine the area more closely. "Don't see it."

Albert shrugged. "You will if you keep rubbing the same spot all day."

"Oh, give me a break." Anthony groaned and flicked the sponge at his twin.

"Hey, watch it. I think I'm going to wear these jeans tonight. Speaking of tonight—you sure you don't want to come with us? We're not doing anything fancy, just burgers and a movie. You might feel better if you come. I mean, Dana and Ethan are going too."

Anthony shook his head. "At the risk of sounding like a grumpy old man, I really don't want to go see a romantic comedy with two couples—one of which is engaged and the other doomed to follow in their footsteps."

Anthony's younger sister, Dana, had been engaged for a little over a month, and already the word wedding was a permanent and repetitive focal point of her vocabulary. Wedding this, wedding that—talking with her and Ethan reminded Anthony of a conversation with a toddler who had just learned a new word.

"And what will you be doing tonight?"

Anthony shot his brother a silencing look. "Man, your car is done. I can finish mine by myself. Don't you have somewhere to go?"

Albert didn't take the hint. "I hate to be pesky, but I don't want to come home and find my dear twin brother on the couch, with his eyes glazed over from an excess of chips, soda, and video games."

Anthony said nothing but hurried to finish rinsing the car. Albert was being way too annoying, and Anthony was ready for some quiet time.

"Maybe I should call Mom—leave an anonymous tip that one of her babies is having a hard time. I'm sure she'd come over and keep you company."

"Don't do it, man. You *will* be sorry if Mom gets all worried about me."

"Look—I just want to make sure you're okay before I go anywhere tonight. Can you at least tell me what your plans are?"

"If you must know, I am going to church. The singles' group is planning to play volleyball in the gym, and I decided I might as well go."

"Good for you. I think you'll have fun."

"I guess. It would be even more fun if Evette would come too. Justin's been back here for only two weeks, and already she's skipped Sunday school and Bible study."

"But she came to Sunday morning service," Albert reminded him. "If you want to see her, why don't you go and set up another golf lesson?"

"Didn't you just say I did the right thing by not kissing her?"

"Yeah, but I didn't say you should never talk to her again. Have you prayed about it?"

Anthony shrugged. "Sort of. Every time I start praying I imagine her and that Justin together. That's what they both want, you know. I could tell by the way they looked at each other. I predict they'll be engaged again by June."

"That's next month."

"Really? I think we should sign you up for genius school."

Albert chuckled and held up his hands in defense. "Okay, that didn't make much sense. I was only trying to keep the conversation going."

Albert glanced at his watch. "Dana and Ethan went shopping for wedding stuff, and I'm supposed to pick up Brienne and meet them in an hour. I'm going to change shirts and leave now. I hope you're in a better mood when I get back."

"I do too."

"Just don't let your thoughts about Evette and Justin stop you from praying. Look at all the examples in the Bible. Moses and David and Joseph and Gideon—what if they had given up because things looked or felt impossible?"

Anthony nodded. "I know you're right. I guess I needed a nudge in that direction."

❧

Evette arrived at church a few minutes early. Not surprisingly she struggled to ignore the butterflies in her stomach.

Coming to the singles' event was a step of faith for her. She'd given in only after several reminder calls from Kaycee Hall, a woman on the hospitality committee.

Glancing around the parking lot as she headed inside, she couldn't help but search for Anthony's car. In the two weeks since Justin's return, she had been too embarrassed to attend Sunday school or Wednesday night services. The circumstances of her parting from Anthony that night at her parents' made her feel uncomfortable, and since she didn't know any of the others in the singles' group that well, she had opted not to go. When he never showed up to schedule another lesson, Evette had simply accepted the fact they weren't meant to be a couple.

But Kaycee had kept after her about the volleyball outing. Yesterday evening Evette hadn't been home when Kaycee called. Her mother had taken a detailed message, though, and almost insisted that Evette go.

"Even if you and Anthony don't ever speak again, why should that keep you away from church? You should go and make other Christian friends," her mother urged.

Evette chose to come this once to give herself a break from her mother's worrying.

She paused outside the gymnasium door and fought the urge to turn around and run home. Strangely enough, she had worked alongside Justin for the last ten days and had not been a bit distracted or angry or even wistful. Yet the possibility that she might see or speak to Anthony tonight made her knees feel weak.

Evette gave herself a quick pep talk. *Don't be silly. You're imagining these emotions. Anthony doesn't care for you like that. He's just glad you're back in church. In fact, he probably thinks of you as his little sister or something.*

Yes, that was it. Wasn't there a verse in the Bible somewhere about that? Something about men treating the women in church like sisters. Evette made a mental note to look it up when she got home. Perhaps that would explain Anthony's intentions.

Feeling momentarily strengthened she swung the door open. Several people were already inside, and Anthony was not one of them.

Evette exhaled the breath she didn't realize she'd been holding. "Thank You, Lord," she whispered.

"What was that?"

Evette didn't have to turn around to know that Anthony had heard her quiet prayer of relief.

"Um, I was only praying." She felt her face grow warm and willed herself not to turn around until after she stopped blushing.

"Let me get that for you."

Anthony rushed forward to hold the door she had already opened.

She stepped inside the gym, and Anthony followed. "Praying about what?" he asked.

"I'd rather not say. Sometimes prayers are just between you and God, you know."

He let out a chuckle. "Yeah. I actually don't know why I even asked. Forget I said that, okay?"

Evette nodded. Anthony looked as handsome as ever, and she felt a pang of regret that things had gone sour between them. She prayed once more, this time taking care not to say anything out loud. *Lord, help me to get over him quickly. I'd like to have fun tonight and not keep going over what-ifs.*

They stood side by side, not speaking but watching the action on the court for several seconds until Kaycee came running over.

"Evette, I was beginning to think you had changed your mind. And, Albert, I thought you said you couldn't come."

"Actually, I'm Anthony," he corrected. "Albert did have another engagement, but I decided to come here."

Kaycee leaned forward and peered at Anthony curiously. "Oh! I guess you are Anthony." Shaking her head she added, "I can never tell you two apart. You should wear name tags or something. Of course, you and your brother are such practical jokers that I wouldn't put it past either of you to pretend to be the other." She giggled then gestured toward the center of the floor. "That game will be ending in a few minutes; then we'll start a new one. Why don't you two come on over and mingle with everyone else?"

"Sounds good to me." Evette followed Kaycee to the other side of the room. It was high time she got to know some of the other people her age who attended this church. Some of them she knew from her younger days, but reestablishing these friendships would still take time.

Although Anthony followed, they spent much of the evening apart, fellowshipping in separate groups.

After the meet-and-greet session, several games of volleyball, and a banana split buffet, everyone sat down on the floor while Gene Harris, the group leader, gave a short lesson.

At first Evette had trouble concentrating. Anthony sat right next to her, and her thoughts jogged back and forth between the man sitting beside her and the content of the lesson.

"Let's all turn in our Bibles to Matthew 22:37," said Gene.

Chagrined, Evette realized she had forgotten her Bible, but Anthony had his and offered to share.

"I'll try to keep this short, so why don't we all read aloud? That way I'll know I have everyone's full attention." Gene laughed, indicating he was trying to keep the mood light-hearted, but Evette wished she could melt into the floor. Was it that obvious that her mind had been wandering?

Feeling her cheeks flame yet again, Evette cleared her throat and read along with the others. "Jesus replied, 'Love the Lord your God with all your heart and with all your soul and with all your mind.' "

Gene closed his Bible. "That's all. Any questions or thoughts you'd like to discuss?"

Evette watched the others in the group. Everyone else seemed as surprised as she felt about the brevity of this lesson.

After several moments and no response from anyone, Gene chuckled softly. "I guess everybody's in shock, since

I'm notoriously long-winded."

The crowd laughed in response, and Gene continued. "I guess I could be obliged to add more to my talk. I wanted to address a problem, or concern, that I'm certain many of you have struggled with from time to time.

"Some of us who are not married enjoy being single. Others are anxiously counting the days until we find our mate. Whether or not they mean to, those around us have the tendency to bring up the topic more often than we'd wish."

Gene paced back and forth, stopping now and then to emphasize a word or phrase. "Even the most steadfast and content singles have days where we feel pangs of loneliness. Usually this group won't seek after romantic relationships but will sit back and see what happens. If someone comes along, good; if no one comes along, then we can deal with that as well. We'll sometimes think back on previous relationships and wonder if we were mistaken when we chose not to pursue marriage earlier in life.

"Then there are some of us who jump from one relationship to the next, searching, second-guessing, analyzing, and often not getting anywhere. These will probably more often feel the pain of breakups and misunderstandings, and sometimes even betrayal."

Evette swallowed hard. She'd had only one real boyfriend, but she could fully sympathize with the agony of what Gene had mentioned. She had given Justin her all, and he had thrown it away. The gaping hole left by what she'd poured into their relationship still ached at the most inopportune times, no matter how hard she tried to ignore it.

Gene's voice broke into her thoughts. "We love Jesus and want to serve Him and give Him our best. I know you've heard that now, while you're still single, is an excellent time to put your all into serving the Lord. Although singleness can seem burdensome at times, the amount of flexibility and freedom you have at this stage can allow you to give more of your time than you could if you were married and raising a family."

Evette had heard this before, and while it made sense, it didn't bring much comfort. She never felt called to preach in foreign lands or quit her job to take on a full-time mission position. Even though she enjoyed her life as a single woman, she couldn't deny that she sometimes felt a longing for marriage and a family. Sometimes she daydreamed of ironing shirts, planning meals, and even changing diapers.

Though her days were no longer consumed with sorrow regarding the end of the engagement, Evette still felt something was missing.

She glanced at Anthony and wondered "what-if" one more time. He must have felt her gaze on him because he turned and gave her a smile.

The fluttery feeling in her stomach returned. But now was not the time for romantic daydreams. Evette pushed the thoughts away and tried to regain her concentration. She glanced up as Gene made eye contact with her.

He must have sensed I wasn't paying attention, Evette decided, feeling sheepish.

Gene cleared his throat and kept going. "My point is simple. Maybe you feel that while you are single you're only a fraction of a person. You hope you'll feel whole—that whatever is missing will magically materialize when you find the right person. I know I've wrestled with these same emotions." He paused and took a drink of water.

Evette shifted slightly and sat up straighter. She didn't want to miss a word of this. She had been mulling over the same thoughts.

"Folks," said Gene, "don't let this idea run your life. You are a whole person. Now don't get me wrong—when you do get married, you will feel another kind of completeness. But to imagine and be concerned that you must meet someone in order to be whole is not correct.

"Love the Lord your God with everything in you—your entire heart, your entire mind, your entire soul. It's not as easy as it sounds. But I can guarantee you this—once you get going, you'll wish you had done it sooner."

He stopped pacing and shrugged. "So you don't have a significant other yet. Don't despair about it. Choose now to serve Jesus with all of your energy. Love Him. He makes you whole. He saved you, He redeemed you, and He loves you. He loves you with all He has, and you can do the same for Him. Give Him your all. Remember those worries about being a fraction of a person?"

Gene shook his head. "Love Jesus with all your mind and don't give those thoughts any room. Does your heart ache sometimes? Open all the empty spaces in your heart, fill them with love for Jesus, and the ache will disappear.

"Be whole in Him. I promise—you'll be so much happier. Even if you don't think you're unhappy, you'll notice the difference. Besides, this is an attitude you want to have in place before you say 'I do.'

"If you don't, Miss or Mr. Right will come along, and you'll feel better for awhile. You'll think he or she was the missing piece. You'll go merrily along, thinking the puzzle is solved. But what happens the day you have a disagreement? Or when the other person disappoints you? What if one of you says something hurtful—and you don't even mean it?

"All of a sudden you might feel that hole open up again, and this time it'll be bigger. You'll be discouraged and may even wonder if you should have stayed single.

"This is when you'll need to realize that no person is perfect and people will fail you. You'll be able to pick up, forgive, and move on with your mate. We all make mistakes.

"So don't put all your trust in people. This doesn't mean you can't have deep and intimate relationships with other people. It simply means you shouldn't look to them to make you feel complete. Please give your all to the One who can make you whole. Make that choice and live it now. Do it while you have the opportunity to practice and grow at it. Pretty soon it'll be second nature to you."

Gene quickly ended in prayer and called the evening to a close.

Evette somehow got to her feet and made her way out to the car, but she didn't remember how. Her mind was still replaying bits and pieces of Gene's lesson.

He had hit the nail on the head—at least for her situation. She had been prepared to let herself believe she'd fallen in love with Anthony because she felt incomplete. Not that he wasn't a nice guy—a solid Christian—good looking. But she wanted more than anything to find some way to plug the crater that had formed when Justin left.

Evette shook her head as she fumbled with her car keys. No, that crater had existed before Justin left. It had existed in college, even in high school. Then one day she looked up and felt a void, a tiny sinkhole of nothingness. Not long afterward, Justin had asked her out, and she accepted happily. The chasm was gone. Sort of.

Gene was right. Time with Justin had filled the gap. But when they argued or were apart for long periods of time or when she mistrusted him, the hollow came back—even bigger.

The time spent in getting over the breakup had caused the

cavity to swell so large that Evette sometimes wondered if it would grow big enough to swallow her.

The delight of getting to know Anthony and a hint of his attraction to her began the cycle once again—a temporary fix for the hollow that quickly faded once she realized her assumptions were incorrect.

Evette located the correct key and unlocked the door. Footsteps sounded behind her. "Evette?"

It was Anthony. She put on a brave smile. "Hi."

He leaned closer. "Are you crying? Is everything okay?"

Evette blinked. She hadn't noticed the pooling tears until Anthony mentioned them. She rubbed her eyes with the back of her hand, thankful the sky was nearly dark. How embarrassing to be caught crying, of all things. "No. Just—watering, I guess. Pollen, maybe."

"Oh. One of my sisters has bad allergies, so I hope you feel better soon." He shifted from one foot to another but didn't say anything.

Evette cleared her throat and looked around. People spilled out of the church, some headed directly to their cars, some in groups of two or more, laughing and talking.

She sensed that Anthony had more he wanted to say, but she wasn't certain she was ready to hear whatever it was.

"Well," she said, taking care to keep her smile intact, "I guess I'll see you at church tomorrow?"

"Yeah. I'll be here. And I was wondering if you wanted to have lunch afterward?"

Evette shook her head. She had too many feelings to sort out. "I don't think so."

"It'll be at my parents' house. We usually all get together for dinner a couple of Sundays out of the month. I know they'd like to meet you." Anthony still sounded hopeful, and she hated to let him down.

"In fact, I know I can't. It's my brother's birthday, and his wife is planning a big party tomorrow afternoon. I really shouldn't miss it." Evette was grateful for the excuse, but declining the invitation still felt bittersweet.

"I see."

Evette slid into her seat. She decided that if he had anything else to say he would spill it before she drove away. As she was closing the door, Anthony spoke up.

"About last week—when I came over. I didn't mean to be rude or harsh when I left. And you're right—I don't know the entire situation, so it's not my place to opine about how Justin should be treated."

Evette didn't know how to read this comment. Did this mean he felt differently about her? She also noticed he had failed to mention the attempted kiss.

"Well, I'm glad you feel that way. Because he's working at the store full time now."

Anthony swallowed then took a deep breath. "I guess I never did reschedule my lesson. Can you fit me in some time this week?"

"Definitely," she smiled. She couldn't help but feel excited at the prospect of spending more time with him. "My schedule is even more flexible right now because Justin's almost always available to work in the shop. Of course that's because he doesn't have many students yet, but for now I can work around your calendar since you've gotten so busy lately." Evette stopped talking and reprimanded herself for rambling. That was a sure sign she was nervous.

"I'm free on Monday. How's two o'clock?"

"Perfect. I'll make a note of it in my planner."

Anthony rested his arm on the roof of her car. "I guess I've kept you standing out here long enough. I'll see you Monday."

Evette smiled. It felt as if things were returning to normal between them, and that was a relief. "I'll see you tomorrow— at church. Remember?"

He laughed. "Oh, yeah. Tomorrow. And if you change your mind about coming to my parents' just let me know. I'll give you a rain check, and you can redeem it whenever you want."

"Will do." Evette closed the door and started the car as Anthony walked away.

The wistful feeling wrung at her heart again. He would make a perfect boyfriend. . .soul mate. . .husband. In a flash she could picture them at their wedding, decorating a home, taking their kids to the park.

Her thoughts returned to Gene's lesson, and she firmly pushed the images away. The ache of emptiness had resurfaced.

Evette closed her eyes and breathed a silent prayer. *Lord, I want to be whole. And not because I have somebody. Show me how I can let You fill those hollow places—because I can't handle the weight of it on my shoulders again.*

eight

The jangling of the doorbell signaled that someone was entering the shop. Evette looked up as Trevor and Craig strolled in.

"Hey, Sis, we're back from lunch," Trevor announced.

Evette laid her paperwork aside. "Good, because I'm famished."

"I suggest the Caribbean chicken salad at Grady Bakeries," said Trevor. "That's what we had."

"I'll keep that in mind."

"How's business?" Craig wanted to know.

"Brisk. This nice weather has given lots of people golf fever. Since you two left, almost everyone who walks in the door has bought balls or gloves or tees."

"Where's everybody else?" Trevor glanced around the shop.

"Dad and Drew are in back rewrapping grips and fitting clubs. I think a couple of people left some clubs to have the shaft changed, and Dad said he'd let one of you handle it."

"Where's Justin?"

"He had his first lesson." Evette glanced at her watch. "He should be finished any minute now."

"Well, good for him. He's a great teacher, and I knew it was only a matter of time before people started beating down the door to study with him," said Craig.

"Yeah," Trevor agreed. "I'll have to watch my students and make sure they don't migrate over to him. I guess that makes him the resident pro around here."

"That makes who the resident pro?" Justin's voice sounded from the back of the store.

Trevor grinned. "Hey, you caught us talking about you. I don't want to look up and find out you took all my students."

Justin laughed. "I don't think we have to worry about that. I'm relieved I finally got one student. I was beginning to wonder."

Evette shook her head. "You didn't have to worry. You're a great teacher. As soon as word gets out, there'll be a throng of people at the door trying to get some range time with you."

"You think so?"

"I know so." Evette's heart did a familiar flip-flop. She had tried very hard to keep her distance from Justin, but that proved more and more difficult when she spent six or eight hours a day in his presence.

He seemed different somehow. Her father and brothers knew more about the reasons behind Justin's sudden return, and she had decided not to ask too many questions. The less she knew, the less she thought about the situation, and that helped her cope with his being around again. But Craig had confided that Justin's failure on the tour had humbled him considerably. His new vulnerability made Evette want to reach out to him and somehow cheer him up. The fact that he had a new student seemed to help considerably.

"Well, since I have this first lesson behind me, I want to celebrate. Who wants to go to lunch with me? It's my treat," said Justin.

"Sorry, but Craig and I just ate," Trevor announced.

"Dad and Drew will probably work through to get those orders filled, so you'll have to do the celebration lunch another day," said Craig.

Justin's shoulders drooped. "Well, what about you, Eve? Have you eaten yet?"

"I was going to run out and get a sandwich, and that's not very festive. Craig's right—you should celebrate another day when everyone can come. An evening would probably be best for everyone."

"Haven't you guys ever heard of spur-of-the-moment? Come on, Eve—don't make me have lunch by myself. I know you can't be upset with me still—I thought we agreed to let bygones be bygones. I know a great restaurant, and we'll be in and out in an hour."

Evette's brothers and Justin were silent as they waited for her answer. True, they had agreed to let the past remain in the past, but that didn't involve going to lunch with him. Still, she supposed it would be harmless, and she hated to be a party pooper when his confidence had a boost.

"Okay, I'll go. But I need to be back by two because I have a lesson."

Justin jingled his keys and glanced at his watch. "Hey, that's almost two hours. Believe me—we have plenty of time."

Before she knew it, Evette found herself in Justin's car as they zoomed toward the restaurant. One thing she hadn't missed about her ex-fiancé was his tendency to drive way too fast. Taking a deep breath Evette checked the tension on her seat belt and prayed they would be safe. She hoped they wouldn't be in the car too long. When Justin entered the freeway, Evette's heart sank. The last thing she needed was to be in midday traffic on Highway 40 with a wannabe race car driver.

"Where are we going?" she ventured.

"This nice little café in the Central West End."

"Central West End? Are you kidding? It takes a good half hour to get there from this part of Chesterfield. I thought you said we'd be in and out in an hour," she protested.

"I changed my mind when you said you needed to be back

by two. We have a little extra time so we might as well make the most of it."

"Isn't there anywhere else we can go?" she pleaded.

He considered for a moment. "I guess we could go to Clayton or Soulard."

Evette leaned back in her seat. She had also forgotten Justin's love for out-of-the-way places. She had once considered this trait romantic, but now she dreaded being in the car with him for more than ten minutes.

Considering her choices carefully, Evette decided the much farther ride to Soulard would fray her nerves too badly. Though Clayton was a bit closer, Justin would probably be upset she didn't want to visit his intended restaurant. "Never mind. We can do the West End."

"Good," said Justin. "I think you'll like it."

They didn't talk much for the remainder of the ride, except for Evette's many warnings for Justin to slow down or look out.

By the time they reached their destination, Evette was grateful Justin had the decency to open her car door. Her legs felt so wobbly from his risk taking that she didn't think she could stand if he *hadn't* taken her arm.

"Are you okay?" he asked.

"Honestly, I don't know. I think you drive even worse than you did when we—" She stopped midsentence, not wanting to say the word engaged.

Justin merely laughed and gave her a quick hug. "Nah. You just drive so slow that you forget what it feels like to go the speed limit."

At least twenty retorts ran through her mind, but Evette held her tongue. After all, this was supposed to be his celebration lunch. She only had to smile and say encouraging things and everything would be fine.

Once they were seated and had ordered their meals, Justin's easygoing demeanor changed somewhat. He grew very serious and leaned across the table to take her hand in his. "Remember what I said about bygones back at the store?"

Evette resisted the urge to pull her hand away. "Yes," she said cautiously.

"I didn't really mean it."

Evette blinked in surprise. Surely he wasn't about to blame her for the entire breakup? In her opinion the fault rested solely on *his* shoulders.

"Don't get me wrong," he explained. "I mean the part about putting the painful things behind us, but I wonder—"

Evette shook her head and took a sip of her water. "Don't wonder. Let's try not to think about it. There's nothing to wonder about."

"Come on, Eve—I know you. I still have feelings for you, and sometimes I can tell by the way you look at me that you do too. I messed up—made some big mistakes, but—"

Evette did pull her hand away. "No. I mean that. My family hired you to work for us, not to pick up where you left off. I don't dislike you, but I have feelings, emotions. I spent all this time trying to rationalize why you left. There's no way we can just—start again."

Justin leaned back in his chair and stared out the window.

Evette suddenly felt cold. "Justin, please. This is supposed to be your big celebration. Let's not be angry with each other—why don't we try to talk about something positive instead?"

After several moments of silence he finally spoke. "You're right. It's been hard for me to be around you every day. I keep thinking about how I ruined everything, and I wonder— you know, if we'd gotten married, next month would be our six-month anniversary."

Evette twisted the napkin in her lap. "Can we please change the subject? Reminiscing about what could have been may be fun and nostalgic for you, but it's not my cup of tea." Her brave front wasn't completely honest. Despite her words Evette had a difficult time suppressing the image of herself as a bride, headed down the aisle to meet Justin.

Justin held up his hands. "No problem. What do you want to talk about?"

"Anything." Evette placed the napkin on the table. "Tell me about life on the tour."

His features darkened. "There's not that much to tell. I couldn't cut it. I'm not the worst, but I'm far from the best." He shrugged. "I was silly to throw myself into it like that. I should have come home, trained some more, married you, and then gone back to give it a shot. I was too impatient, and the more I tried to fix my game, the more it fell apart."

The pitiful expression on his face nearly moved her to tears. It was so easy to be unconcerned about him when he wasn't sitting right in front of her. "Then I'm glad you came back. Who knows—maybe you can try again in another year or so."

"Or maybe not. I'm not so sure that's what I want." His voice was urgent, almost pleading. "Maybe I'm meant to be a teacher, not a pro. I think I want to settle down, raise a family, you know."

The sound of Justin talking about raising a family rendered Evette speechless for the moment. Was he intentionally trying to make her cry?

"Are you okay?" he asked for the second time since they'd arrived.

Evette closed her eyes for several moments to hold back the tears. They weren't tears of either joy or sadness; instead they sprang from a mixture of emotions—emotions she didn't feel capable of processing.

For Justin to saunter back into her life and suggest they start over was too good to be true. There had to be a catch—some kind of conditional promise. *Yes, that's it. He wants something.*

Satisfied with her analysis Evette opened her eyes. She wouldn't let his hints and insinuations get next to her. "I'm fine," she told him.

At that moment the waitress arrived, bearing their lunches. Feeling rattled from the wave of emotions, Evette took a bite of her salad right away. Then she noticed Justin hadn't started eating.

"Did they get your order wrong?"

"No, I was just wondering if you wanted me to say grace?"

Justin wanted to say grace? That was a first. In the past he had grudgingly paused as Evette said a short blessing over the food. But after awhile she had given up completely.

Now she blushed deeply, having been caught skipping grace. *By him, of all people.*

Evette wanted to groan. She'd so wanted to show Justin how much she had changed, how she'd grown closer to the Lord, how she didn't need a mate to be whole—how she was better off without him. Now he'd gotten her on a technicality.

She wiped her mouth with the napkin and nodded. "I guess I forgot about praying over the meal."

"That's okay." Justin reached across the table for her hand. "Do you mind if I—?"

Evette shook her head. "No, go ahead." She bowed her head as Justin prayed a very short, but eloquent prayer.

He began eating, but she couldn't think clearly. She was impressed, to say the least.

He must have felt her watching him because he stopped eating. "Something wrong?"

"No, not really. I admit I'm surprised to hear you praying. You didn't care for things like that before. Do you mind my asking when this changed?"

He hesitated. "It's kind of personal, but I guess I was lonely out there by myself. I think one day I simply felt as if I needed to find out more about God." He shrugged. "It kind of reminded me of you in a way. I felt—I don't know—secure."

Evette listened while he talked. His comments were pretty generic, but she did sense that he was searching for a spiritual change. She thought carefully. In all honesty she couldn't remember if Justin had ever accepted Jesus into his heart. He'd attended church off and on, but other than that he didn't seem too interested in anything having to do with the Lord.

Of course, that didn't prove whether or not a person had a relationship with the Lord. Evette could attest to that. Only recently had she decided to focus on Jesus and live her life for Him.

Now that she had lived both sides of the story, she likened being a halfhearted Christian to being a halfhearted runner or golfer. It wasn't optimal. When she had played sports in school, she had learned quickly that slacking off in her training made for poor performance in the competitive arena. The same went for spending time with the Lord every day, instead of only on Sundays.

In real sports, when Evette's body was strong, she was less susceptible to game-day injuries. In the same way a well-fed spirit protected her from spiritual injuries. In the short period since she had resumed a daily quiet time, Evette already felt more well rounded. *I feel whole.*

"I felt as if I was missing something," Justin admitted. "I never liked church that much, but the few times I went, I felt that I was getting in on something I needed."

Evette nodded excitedly. Now was her chance to share her own progress. "I know exactly how you feel. The pastor at church talked a bit about this yesterday."

"Really? What did he say?"

Evette was definitely surprised now. The old Justin would never have voluntarily asked for a sermon synopsis. She plunged ahead. "Well, the Scripture he spoke about was in 1 Corinthians chapter 9. It compares a person's walk with the Lord to training for a race. I guess I identified with that since I ran track in school."

Evette stopped to be certain Justin was still listening. "The point is—you have to approach your life as though you're getting ready to run a big race. You have to keep your goal in sight. You can't just 'kind of' do things, but you have to be as dedicated to this life in Christ as a person training for the Boston Marathon is to winning."

Justin nodded. "I've never thought about things in that light before. But I'm impressed with what you know."

"What do you mean?"

"I mean, you've been going to church all these years, and I went only when I was forced to. Now that I'm at this kind of crossroad in my career and everything, I wish I'd paid more attention to sermons and prayer meetings."

She chuckled. "It's not too late. Trust me on this. Why don't you come to church with me sometime? Or even Wednesday night classes? It may feel a little awkward at first—it did for me. But once you get into it, you'll be so surprised at how much you start to understand the Bible."

He shrugged. "I don't know. It sounds kind of interesting. Let me think about it, and I'll let you know."

"Sure."

Justin grinned. "You know, all this talk about the Bible reminds me of back when we first started dating. You used to go to those Bible camps and everything. Do you remember the time when—"

nine

"Are you sure she remembered my lesson?" Anthony paced back and forth inside the pro shop. It didn't seem like Evette to forget about his class. And her brothers seemed to be deliberately holding back part of their explanation as to where she was. A two-hour lunch break seemed a little far-fetched in his opinion.

"I know she remembered because she mentioned it before she went to lunch," Craig answered. "It's only ten after two so they may have gotten stuck in traffic."

The last sentence caught Anthony's attention. "They?" This was the first he'd heard of Evette having left with another person.

The phone rang, and Craig answered it hurriedly. As he spoke, he motioned for Anthony to take a seat or browse the shop. Anthony decided on the latter.

Moments later the bell on the door announced an entry. Before he saw her, he heard Evette's laughter.

A feeling of dread washed over him as he caught a glimpse of her walking in, her arm looped through Justin's. She seemed a little unsteady on her feet, but if she was hurt she probably wouldn't be laughing. Feeling awkward, Anthony hung back and remained where he stood.

"I will never ride in a car with this man again," she told Craig.

"Still has a lead foot, huh?"

"Lead is putting it mildly. Is there a heavier adjective we could use?"

"Let me remind you that you were the one complaining about being late for your lesson. I did my best to get you here on time," Justin said.

"Next time, let me be late."

"You are late," Craig pointed out. "I'm putting you two on record for the longest lunch break in history."

"Sorry," Evette said. "We started talking about the old days when we were kids and. . ." Her voice trailed off as she stared at Craig. "You said I was late for my lesson. Did Anthony show up?"

"Ahem." Anthony stepped out into clear view. "I was here five minutes early even."

"Oh, no." Evette covered her face with her hands. "I'm so sorry. Of course I'll deduct part of the cost. Let me grab my clubs, and I'll meet you out on the range." Before he could answer, she disappeared into the back room.

Anthony hefted his bag onto his shoulder. "I guess the lesson starts now."

Justin stepped forward and held out his hand. "I know we met briefly, but we weren't properly introduced. I'm Justin Greene."

"Anthony Edwards. Evette tells me you're an old family friend." Anthony felt a degree of satisfaction from using the word *friend*. That sounded so much better than ex-fiancé. He didn't like the idea of Evette's spending time with this guy, no matter how long ago the wedding had been called off.

Anthony couldn't shake the mental image of how natural the two of them had seemed together moments earlier.

"Anthony Edwards—don't you write a sports column for the newspaper?"

Anthony nodded. "Yeah, I sure do. It's been nice meeting you, but if you'll excuse me, I need to get my lesson in. I'd hate to miss out on more time than I already have." He turned and walked toward the exit that led to the driving range.

"I'll see you around," Justin called after him.

I hope not, Anthony thought.

Evette waited for him outside. "I'm so sorry you had to wait. Justin taught his first lesson today, and he wanted to celebrate. Craig and Trevor had already eaten, and Dad and Drew were busy, so he talked me into going." She paused but kept looking directly at him. "I felt as if I should go, you know, because he's been a little depressed about not doing well on the tour, and I wanted to cheer him up—boost his confidence some. I thought we were going to a place nearby, but he wanted to go to the Central West End. It was either there or Clayton or Soulard—so I picked the West End, since that's where he wanted to go in the first place. Then we got to talking and eating, and I totally lost track of time."

He set his bag down and pulled out the pitching wedge. "We start with this one, right?"

"Right. And you're sure you're not upset about my being late?"

This was not a topic he felt comfortable discussing at the moment. Nor was this a good place. He would prefer to take her out to dinner and find out whether or not he had a chance at a deeper relationship than they now shared.

He did his best to remain lighthearted. "Look—you don't have to answer to me. You don't have to give me a full report of where you've been or what you've done—because we don't have that kind of relationship."

She blinked slowly. "Of course I know that," she said in a voice that sounded overly cheerful. "I just wanted you to know that—"

Anthony shook his head. "Evette, nobody's perfect. I can't

say I've never missed an appointment or run late. And if you feel as if you need to help your friend get his confidence back, then don't let me stop you."

She bit her lip and looked away. Anthony wished he could rewind the time and take back everything he'd just said. *She's genuinely concerned about Justin, and all I can do is think about my own hurt feelings.*

Anthony considered the distance between the two of them. In two short steps he could have her in his arms.

"For some reason this feels pretty awkward, doesn't it?" Evette asked suddenly.

Anthony nodded. "Yeah. I guess I should admit I'm not too happy about your getting back together with the man you nearly married. I was hoping maybe we were getting to be more than friends."

Anthony heard the door squeak open as Evette was about to answer. He could tell from the look on her face they were no longer alone on the range.

To his great frustration he turned around to find Justin lugging his clubs down the corridor. The man had the nerve to take up residence on the practice mat next to the one where Anthony stood.

"I didn't know you had another lesson today," Evette remarked.

"Nah. I don't have another one. But things are slow inside so I thought I'd come out and work on my long game for a bit."

"Oh." Neither Evette nor Anthony moved as Justin began a warm-up.

Anthony looked to Evette for help. Justin could have chosen at least twenty other practice mats, and in Anthony's opinion his current choice bordered upon rude.

"Do you think you could move down a bit?" Evette suggested. "I'm giving a lesson, and—"

"Oh, I see." Justin gave her a knowing look. "Afraid he might hit a bad shot? I better move for my own safety, huh?"

Evette cleared her throat but didn't answer that question directly. "I'd just like to have a little student-teacher privacy, if you don't mind."

"Not a problem." Justin grabbed his bag and moved all of one space over.

Anthony wanted to groan, and Evette didn't look very pleased. She opened her mouth to say something, but Anthony decided it would be best to leave well enough alone. "Never mind," he said quietly. "Let's get started."

Evette had him review his swing motion then let him start hitting some balls. Not unexpectedly, he did miserably. Anthony did his level best not to shank the ball toward Justin—no way would he give him the satisfaction. But his shots went anywhere but straight.

Whiff, slice, hook, shank, top—you name it; I've mastered every bad shot known to golfers, he thought to himself. But even more annoying was the fact that just ten feet in front of him Justin had settled into a rhythm of great shot after shot after shot.

As soon as Anthony messed up, Justin, without fail, hit the most spectacular drive.

After fifteen minutes Anthony sensed that Justin was only out there to have a laugh at his expense. He stopped and watched Justin hit a few.

"He has a great long game, doesn't he?"

Anthony shrugged but grudgingly agreed. "Yeah, I guess so."

When he resumed practicing, Anthony did even worse than at first, if that was possible. Justin's presence had definitely robbed him of any semblance of progress. Evette must have felt so as well.

"Why don't we work on your putting?" she suggested.

Anthony could have hugged her for being so intuitive. "You'll get no argument from me there." He replaced the clubs and followed her to the putting green.

Justin glanced up as they passed him. "Giving up so soon? That's no way to learn the game. It takes time, and you won't learn to drive by quitting."

Anthony inhaled deeply, trying not to say anything he might later regret. If there were academy awards for being annoying, this man would win.

"No one's given anything up," Evette said. "We're going to putt. Why don't you join us?"

Justin hesitated. "I may do that. I'll check inside, though, to make sure I'm not needed."

Anthony frowned. Did she have to invite Justin along? As soon as they were out of hearing range, he voiced the question to Evette.

"Trust me—he's not going to come. He'll find something to do inside."

"I hope so."

Evette sat down on a chair and covered her face with her hands. "Oh, boy, I shouldn't have said that. I ought to go apologize."

Anthony stopped practicing and knelt beside her. "What are you talking about?"

Her shoulders sagged. "What I said to him about putting. I said it on purpose because I was upset. I felt as if he was trying to wreck your lesson—to get you off balance. I knew you were getting frustrated, and I wanted to make him stop."

Anthony swallowed a smile. It felt good to know that

Evette wanted to spare his feelings. "I still don't understand, though. Why is that so bad?"

Evette shook her head and lowered her voice a bit. "That's why he came back to St. Louis. He's awesome off the tee and in the fairway, but his short game has totally fallen apart. He can't putt for anything. He's trying to relearn, but he doesn't have much confidence right now.

"Since he did his best to show you up on the range, I couldn't resist tossing out a challenge here on the green. I knew he wouldn't show up because there's no way he'd embarrass himself like that. My brothers have already told him how good you are at this."

Anthony felt a surge of pride to find he was better than Justin at something, but his heart went out to Evette, who was caught in the middle somehow.

"I need to tell him I'm sorry," she repeated. "I know I hurt him."

"Don't you think it might hurt his ego that much more if you go in there and apologize for crushing it?"

"Do you think so?"

Anthony shrugged. "I guess not. If I were Justin, I'd feel embarrassed at first, but after awhile I'd be happy you thought enough of me to do that."

"Are you sure?"

He nodded. "Positive."

Evette stood slowly. "I think we can both agree this session has been a near disaster. Let's pretend it didn't happen and schedule you another lesson. I won't charge you a cent for this."

"I don't mind paying. I mean, I feel guilty about taking up your time."

"No. I can't let you pay. We'll pick an hour when Justin isn't here, or I'll make sure my brothers keep him away next time."

"I like that plan," he agreed. Before Evette could get away or change the subject, Anthony reached out and held her hand.

"Remember what we were discussing before he barged in?"

"Yes." Her voice wasn't much louder than a whisper.

"Let me take you to dinner so we can have some time to talk."

For a moment she nodded her head. Then she backed away from him. "I can't. Don't take this personally, but I'm trying to do things right from now on."

"What?" Anthony felt completely bewildered.

"Do you remember what Gene talked about Saturday?"

"Yeah—but I don't understand why you think we can't have dinner. It's just a date. We'll never get to know each other if all we do is golf lessons."

"I know. But maybe now isn't a good time. It's not that I don't want to spend more time with you, because I am attracted to you. I think very highly of you, and I'm honored you asked me out—"

"But what?" Anthony persisted.

"I'm one of those people Gene talked about. I feel that emptiness, and I've always figured that when Mr. Right came along, it would go away. When I dated Justin, I felt better; but when he left, it got worse. When you started paying attention to me, the same thing happened. I think you're a great guy, but what if we aren't meant to be together?"

Anthony didn't answer. He didn't like the direction this conversation was taking.

Evette continued. "Anthony, we'll have to pray about taking our relationship further. But right now I owe it to myself to learn how to be whole in Jesus instead of waiting for the perfect guy to help me feel complete."

Anthony sighed. "I don't like what this means, but I understand and respect what you're doing. I don't have a right to try to distract you from your relationship with God."

She gave him a wry smile. "Isn't that the reason you started bugging me to come to church more often? You obviously thought I needed to polish my halo a bit."

Anthony grinned sheepishly. "Yeah, I guess that's what I said. I have to admit, though, that I was pretty interested in finding out if you might be that someone I could spend the rest of my life with." He gave her his most hopeful look.

She giggled. "Come on—don't make me answer that right now. Give me some time to get my priorities straight, and then we can see about—anything more."

"Okay. I can't promise I won't ever be impatient, but I will wait." He brushed her cheek lightly with his fingertips. "I'll wait for as long as you need."

ten

"The float trip? I don't think so." Evette lifted her eyebrows. A couple of women from Sunday school class had gotten together for lunch and were discussing an upcoming group event.

Nina laughed. "Why not? It's a chance to be in the great outdoors. For somebody who spends so much time outside, you sure don't seem very enthusiastic."

"A manicured golf course is a good deal different from a wild river," Evette countered.

"Come on—you have to go. We need to have an even amount of people so the canoes won't be lopsided," said Michelle.

Evette shook her head. "Sorry, ladies, but this doesn't sound very fun to me. Besides, you won't know if you'll have an uneven number until the sign-up deadline."

Michelle leaned an elbow on the table and rested her chin in her hand. "And the translation for that would be: You want to make sure a certain Mr. Edwards is going before you say yes. Am I right?"

Evette was speechless for a moment. How should she answer that?

Nina laughed. "Uh, oh, she's tongue-tied. I think you're right, Michelle."

Evette finally shook her head. "No, that's not it. Anyway, what are you trying to say about Anthony?"

"We're not saying anything—except we notice you seem

to spend a lot of time talking to him, and he always manages to find a way to sit next to you. People are starting to think of you two as a couple."

"Well, that's not necessarily true."

"So, if someone else is interested in him, you wouldn't be offended?" asked Nina.

Evette sighed. She had suspected Nina liked Anthony, and now she was at a loss. Was it fair to keep other women away from him while she waited on an answer from the Lord? As much as she hoped that one day she and Anthony could have a more serious relationship, Evette felt that being dishonest with Nina would be the equivalent of taking the matter into her own hands, rather than letting the Lord resolve it. "I guess I don't have a clear answer. We've talked about dating, but right now I don't feel ready to move in that direction."

Nina looked puzzled. "So is that a yes or a no?"

"A no, I suppose. We're both attracted to each other, but we mutually agreed not to date."

"I see," said Nina, but the look on her face indicated otherwise. "If I'm not being too presumptuous here—does it have anything to do with that very handsome man who's been coming to church with you lately?"

Evette blushed. How could she explain this without opening every detail of her life to these women? While they had begun a friendship, she didn't feel close enough to them to tell them everything about herself.

"Not really," she told them. "Justin and I are old friends—in fact, several people at church probably remember him from a few years ago. To make a long story short, we were engaged, we broke up, he moved away, but he moved back last month—and right now he works at my dad's store."

"Does he have a girlfriend?" Michelle wanted to know.

"Honestly, I don't know. We don't get that involved in each other's personal lives these days."

Michelle grinned. "Well, be sure to bring him Sunday, and I'll see if *he* wants to go on the float trip."

Evette chuckled. "Are we still discussing the float trip?"

"Come on, Girl," said Nina. "We're talking about the Niangua River. I've done this before, and it's not terribly intimidating. I mean, you're not going to hit any major rapids or anything like that."

Evette sighed. "Okay. How long do I have to make up my mind? Isn't the trip at the end of August?"

"Yes. But you have to decide by the first of August. It's the first week in June now so you have two months to think about it."

"Okay. I'll think about it, but no promises," Evette said firmly.

🕭

Evette was on her stationary bike when the cellular phone rang. Happy for a distraction, she reached for the phone. "Hello?"

"Hi, it's Anthony."

"Oh, hi."

He was quiet for a moment. "Are you jogging or something?"

She laughed. "No. I'm sitting on this bike trying to eke out the last half mile."

"Oh. Then I'm sorry to interrupt."

"Don't worry about it. Besides, there's nothing good on TV, so I was in the process of making up excuses for why I shouldn't finish my workout. Your call is a welcome diversion."

"Good, because I have a favor to ask."

"Ask away." Evette slowed the pace of her pedaling so she could hear better.

"You remember my sister Dana and her fiancé Ethan?"

Evette smiled. "Yes, we've run into each other a few times at church. And Ethan is so charming. What woman doesn't dream of marrying a man who loves to cook?"

"Ahem. Are you taking a shot at my cooking abilities?"

"I don't know. You've never cooked for me."

He laughed. "Trust me—you don't want me to either. Albert says he'd starve if he didn't cook for us."

"That's really sad. Even my brothers can cook in a pinch. My mom made sure of it."

"Yeah, my mom tried to teach me too, but I guess I wasn't paying much attention. But since Albert was a model student in the Mavis Edwards Academy of Culinary Arts, I didn't have to put forth much effort. He cooks, and I eat."

Evette shook her head. "Getting back to this favor—"

"Yes. Remember that Ethan's opening his own restaurant?"

"Mm-hm." Evette leaned forward and pedaled a bit faster. *Just one quarter of a mile to go.*

"Well, they're having a preview party for friends, family, and investors next week. I wondered if you might like to be my guest for the evening."

"This sounds like a serious event," Evette mused aloud. "Is your family expecting you to show up with—anyone?"

"I don't know. I guess they'd be surprised, but I really think it would be good for you to meet them all. Even my brother Max is driving in from Kansas City."

"Aren't he and his wife expecting a baby soon?"

"The end of this month. Of course, my mom thinks they should stay put. She told Max, 'If that baby decides to come early, what will you do?' " Anthony laughed. "Right now she's convinced the baby will be born in the car on the side of I-70. Believe me, she's not too happy about it."

"But they're coming anyway?"

"For now they're holding to the plan. Plus, Stacy's sister Maddy's fiancé has some work in an art show here the same weekend, and they wanted to be here for that too. I think they'll bring Maddy and Jordan to the party with them."

"Wow! This sounds as if it's shaping up to be an exciting event."

"Is that a yes?" Anthony wanted to know.

"I guess so. As long as we don't have to say we're a couple or anything very official. I'd rather be seen as your friend right now."

"Okay, we'll tell them that. But I won't promise that will stop any of them from speculating."

Evette grinned. "I understand. My brothers would do the same. But, to answer your question, I will go."

"Thanks a lot. I'm looking forward to it."

"Me too." Evette glanced at her watch. "I have to run and get ready for work. I have a couple of lessons to teach, and my dad has been hinting that we need to do inventory. Seems he found some inconsistencies in Trevor's method."

"Uh-oh, that sounds like some serious overtime."

"Exactly. Don't panic if you don't hear from me for two or three days."

"The same goes for me. A couple of the guys at work are on vacation so everyone has extra assignments."

"So no golf lessons this week?"

"I doubt it—although Dana's wedding is getting closer, and I want to be able to play with dignity by then."

From the drop in his voice Evette could tell he was getting discouraged.

"Drew told me he's been using a new swing gadget with some of his students, and it seems to work well. Next time you come in, maybe we'll see if it can help you."

"That sounds great. I need to get going, but I'll see you at church. And I'll get back with you next week with more details about this opening."

"Okay." Evette hung up the phone and smiled happily. Although it was sometimes frustrating that she didn't feel a release to be Anthony's girlfriend, it was nice to know he was there for her as a friend. She recognized that other women were interested in him, but he had decided to keep praying and wait for Evette to make her decision.

Now that he wanted her to meet his entire family, she thought all the more highly of him. She also felt more than a bit nervous. *Please, Lord, don't let me make the wrong decision.*

➴

"Okay, how do I look?" Evette twirled in her ankle-length royal blue dress and waited for Anthony's approval.

"You look fantastic. I can't wait to show you off to everyone."

The two of them said good-bye to her parents and walked out to his car. After they drove off, Evette admitted to Anthony that she was extremely nervous. "What if they don't like me?"

He laughed. "Most of them already know you—at least they've seen you at church. I can't think of any reason why they wouldn't like you."

"What about the ones I haven't met?"

He reached over and covered her hand with his, patting it gently. "Relax. It's a party, and everyone will be in a good mood. You don't have to worry about saying the right thing. Just be yourself, and they'll see what I already see in you."

"I'll try my best."

The ride to Ethan's restaurant was far too short for Evette. The butterflies in her stomach were in full force by the time Anthony led her inside.

Dana met them as soon as they walked in. After hugging them both, she turned to Anthony. "You won't believe this, but I think Otis is about to challenge one of our investors to a basketball game."

Anthony shook his head. "Good old Otis. Always trying to get a competition going."

"And you have to stop him," Dana said emphatically.

"Me? Why not Jackson or Albert or somebody?"

"Jackson's not here yet, and Albert is over in the corner with Brienne, looking all googly-eyed. I hate to try to drag him away from her."

Anthony cleared his throat. "I brought someone too, in case you didn't notice."

"I know you did." Dana looped her arm through Evette's. "And I'll take good care of her. I'm going to introduce her to the girls."

Anthony looked at Evette and held up his hands. "I think I'm backed into a corner."

She gave him a brave smile. "I'll be fine."

"All right then." He turned back to his sister. "What do I have to do?"

Dana shrugged. "Get over there and change the subject. Get them talking about something else besides sports. Ethan's in the kitchen cooking his heart out, and he'd be mortified to know that one of my brothers is out here attempting to organize an impromptu tournament. I mean, look at them—they're all wearing suits. And not one of those men is under the age of forty. I seriously doubt any one of them has the game he's bragging about. You have to calm them down before somebody goes out and gets hurt."

Anthony frowned. "I'll do my best. But for future reference tell Mr. Ethan he shouldn't have told Otis about that basketball goal in the back parking lot."

"Come with me," Dana said to Evette. In a matter of moments she ushered her over to a corner table where several women had gathered.

"Ladies, I want to introduce you to someone. This is Anthony's good friend, Evette. She goes to our church so most of you have probably seen her. Just for a refresher, let me go over the names. These are my sisters, Sheryl and Latrice. My sisters-in-law Verna, Marva, and Stacy. Then we have Stacy's sister Maddy, my mother Mavis, my aunt Florence, and my aunt Daphne."

Evette smiled and acknowledged each woman. *I only hope I can keep all of these names straight.*

Mavis Edwards was the first to speak. "Honey, why don't you sit down?" There was an empty seat between her and her daughter-in-law Stacy, and the women gestured for Evette to take that chair.

Feeling nervous because they were all watching her, Evette did her best not to trip in her three-inch heels as she made her way to the spot.

As soon as Evette sat down, Dana said, "Ya'll take good care of her, or else Anthony will be fussing at me for years to come." She winked at Evette. "From what I can tell, I think she's a pretty special friend of his." She checked her watch. "Oops! I think I was supposed to pull something out of the oven five minutes ago. I hope Ethan caught it." In a flash she was headed toward the kitchen.

The first few moments after Dana left, Evette felt awkward. The group had been chatting away until she joined them. She felt like a high-school student trying to barge her way into the cheerleaders' inner circle. They all seemed to be sizing her up.

Finally Stacy leaned over and said in a stage whisper, "Mavis might look stern, but she's a real softie. And the rest of us don't bite, so you can relax."

This comment made everyone laugh, and before she knew it Evette started to feel like one of the girls. "Is this your first big Edwards family event?" Stacy asked. With a shrug she added, "You'll have to excuse me if I ask questions everyone already has answers for. I live on the other side of the state so I miss out on things sometimes."

Evette smiled. She liked Stacy already. "Yes, this is my first official family gathering. I guess you can all tell I'm pretty nervous."

"You should have seen me when Max brought me to meet everyone. I was shaking in my boots. To make matters worse, Mavis put me to the test."

Sheryl laughed. "I had forgotten all about that. Mama made Stacy help clean chitlins." She shook her head.

"Honey, in my kitchen, if you don't clean 'em, you don't eat 'em," Mavis said. "And how was I supposed to know she had never cleaned them before?"

Florence spoke up. "I remember that day. After five minutes anyone could see that child had no idea what she was doing. Mavis, dear, I think you let her keep going on purpose."

"Maybe I did. It was kind of funny to watch."

"It wasn't funny for me," Stacy cut in. "I was miserable. But I guess I deserved it since I was too scared to admit I had no idea what I was doing."

Latrice laughed. "Evette, the moral of the story is, if Mama asks you to do something and you don't know how, just tell her. It'll save you a lot of stress."

"I know that's right," said Daphne. "Mavis is as sweet as honey most of the time, but every once in awhile she likes to play jokes on people."

Mavis stood up and put her hands on Evette's shoulders. "Ya'll need to stop scaring this girl. I declare, this child is shaking." She kissed Evette on the cheek. "Don't pay attention to them. I do have my practical joke streak, but I only do that to people I know well."

Evette smiled, not sure how to handle all the attention. Mavis sat down and folded her hands in her lap. "Of course, since I hear that my Anthony thinks so highly of you, I expect we'll be seeing a lot of each other." Mavis took a deep breath, creating an atmosphere of expectation. "So you might want to watch out when I get to feeling antsy. I do love a good joke."

Daphne shook her head. "She gets creative about it too. One time she even called me on the phone pretending she was selling something."

Verna laughed. "Not just anything, mind you. She got me with that one too. Claimed she was selling tickets for a ride in a time machine."

"That's a new one to me," said Florence. "Now, Mavis, you are too old to be playing like that."

Mavis giggled, looking very much like a schoolgirl. "See, Florence—that's what keeps me young. You ought to try it sometime. I have to let loose every once in awhile and have some fun. I can't let being old stop me, can I, Evette?"

"Um, I guess not," Evette said, hoping she'd come up with the right answer.

"I like you already," Mavis said.

Evette breathed a sigh of extreme relief.

&

Anthony watched Evette from the other side of the restaurant. She seemed to be relaxed and having a good time. He wished he could go over and check on her, but the situation with Otis wasn't quite under control. Both Otis and Mr. Davis had competitive personalities, and it had taken a great deal of time and finesse to smooth the rift between them. Apparently one of the two had asked about the other's skill on the court, and within minutes a simple question had escalated into a challenge of who was the best.

Right now they were discussing football, and while Anthony wished he could veer the conversation away from sports, he took comfort in the fact that there was no football field nearby.

"Hey, little bro." Anthony turned and found Max standing behind him. "It's been awhile since we've seen each other. I missed you." He pulled Anthony into a hug.

"Hey, I missed you too. I've been meaning to come up to Kansas City and visit sometime."

"Good idea. Come in a month or two. By then we'll probably be in desperate need of help. We'll take a couple of days off and let you get up when the baby cries in the middle of the night."

"You excited?"

Max nodded emphatically. "We can't wait."

"I'm guessing Mom is a little surprised her prediction didn't come true."

"Yeah, but Stacy and I are thrilled the baby wasn't born on the side of the highway."

"I know I've already told you this, but I'll say it again. Congratulations."

"Thanks. So now that Sheryl and Dana are engaged"—he glanced toward the corner table where Albert and Brienne sat—"and Albert will pop the question to Brienne any day now, that leaves you. By any chance will I get to meet this Evette that Dana mentioned?"

"I brought her with me, but the women have her now."

Anthony pointed to the table where the female members of his family had congregated. "I'll be lucky if I get to say more than two sentences to her before the night is over. You know how they get when they're all together."

Max nodded. "We're staying the whole weekend so maybe we can get together before we leave."

"That sounds fun, but it all depends on what Evette's schedule is like. I'm not sure if she has classes to teach."

"That's right. She's a golf teacher."

"She's my golf teacher. I need all the help I can get before Ethan takes the groomsmen out to the course."

Max nodded. "I need to brush up on my game too. We've been running around, getting things ready for the baby, and my game hasn't been a priority."

"Does that mean you guys are coming for Dana's wedding for sure?"

"Oh, yeah. I can't miss my baby sister's wedding. And we'll be back in December when Sheryl and Peter get married— same goes for Albert and Brienne. So what's your date?"

"My date?"

"Yeah. Have you and Evette set a date?"

Anthony blinked. "We're not even engaged. Hey, we're not even officially dating."

"Back up and run that by me again. If she's not your girlfriend, then why the buzz on the family grapevine?"

Anthony shrugged. "Because that's how the family grapevine works. Sometimes stuff that isn't news, is, and stuff that's real news gets overlooked."

"Yeah, you're right. But explain to me why everyone is confused about this?"

"I guess it's partially my fault. Evette doesn't want to commit to a romantic relationship right now. She wants to make sure she is spiritually ready to handle a relationship. Plus, her ex-fiancé called off the wedding, moved out of town for several months, and then resurfaced a couple of months ago. I don't think she's still interested in him, but he seems bent on making it difficult for me to spend any time alone with her. He rides to church with her, he hangs around while I'm having my lessons—and she doesn't really do anything to stop him."

Max tilted his head to the side. "Have you two discussed this?"

"You sound exactly like Albert. And, no, we haven't addressed this situation directly. I don't want her to feel as if I'm trying to push her into a decision."

Max nodded solemnly. "I think it might be in order at least to ask for an update. Do you think she's considering going back to the other guy?"

"I hope not. He's so obnoxious that I can't imagine they would make a good couple. But then again she seems intrigued that he's interested in making some spiritual changes, so—"

"Maybe she sees something you don't, or can't, see."

"That's not a happy thought, man."

"And that's exactly why you need to have a talk with her. The sooner, the better. Even if she hasn't made a decision about the two of you, I think you deserve to know if this other man has somehow edged into the running."

"You're right. I will."

"And soon. Promise me that," Max persisted. "Just by looking at you, I can tell you've already fallen for her. I don't want to see you get hurt."

"Me either," Anthony agreed.

≈

The meal was scrumptious—roast duck, salad nicois, spinach soufflé, and mushroom risotto, followed by raspberry and lemon sorbet-filled profiteroles, that looked like tiny cream puffs, for dessert. Ethan was an excellent cook, and everyone agreed his restaurant would be a great success.

But Evette had a difficult time enjoying herself because she sensed something different about Anthony. When they arrived, he had been jovial and lighthearted; but now he seemed terribly quiet and contemplative.

Did I do something to upset him? Did I say something wrong? she wondered.

Before she could give the matter any more thought, the party took an unexpected turn. Stacy whispered something to her husband, Max, and in a flash he jumped out of his seat.

For the next few minutes everyone ran around trying to be of assistance, but mostly getting in the way, as Max put his wife into the car and headed to the nearest hospital. The newest member of the Edwards clan had decided to come two weeks ahead of schedule.

eleven

"Evette, wake up." Evette could hear Anthony's voice, but it sounded far away—almost as if she were in a tunnel somewhere.

Where am I? She opened her eyes only to squeeze them shut again. *Some place with really harsh lighting,* she decided. She opened her eyes again but blinked rapidly in hopes of giving them a few moments to adjust.

"I have another nephew," Anthony said, beaming. "It's a boy."

The hospital. Now I remember. Stacy had the baby. She stifled a yawn and smiled. "Congratulations. Have you seen him yet?"

"Just for a couple of minutes. He's so little."

Evette couldn't help but smile. "Most babies are. When was he born?"

"About twenty minutes ago."

Evette checked her watch. "I can't believe it's seven in the morning."

"And I can't believe you slept through the birth."

She shook her head. "I missed all of the excitement."

"It wasn't that exciting. All we did was sit out here and wait."

"Was I the only one who fell asleep?"

"Dad dozed off for awhile, but everyone else stuck it out."

Evette's face grew warm. "I guess I was pretty conspicuous." She buried her face in her hands. "I didn't realize I was so tired—I remember calling my parents when we got here to let them know what was happening—but I don't remember falling asleep. How embarrassing."

Anthony rubbed her shoulders. "Don't worry about it. We all took turns letting you lean on us."

Evette wanted to groan. "Double embarrassment," she muttered. "Please tell me I did not drool or snore."

Anthony cleared his throat and looked away, but not before she saw him swallow a big grin.

"Oh, no," she wailed softly. She glanced around the nearly empty waiting room. "Where is everyone?"

"Standing in front of the observation window oohing and aahing over him."

"Ohh, how sweet."

"Do you want to see him?"

"Yes and no. I'm too embarrassed to face everyone."

Anthony stood and held out his hand. "Not a good excuse. There's no reason to feel like that. You had a long week, and you were worn out. So you fell asleep. Big deal. Everyone goes to sleep. I won't let you feel ashamed about it."

Evette placed her hand in Anthony's. "All right."

"All right," Anthony echoed. "Let's go see this baby."

The entire family huddled together outside the nursery window.

Amazing how new babies put everyone in a good mood— even people who haven't slept a wink all night, Evette mused.

Anthony maneuvered a corner spot for Evette and him. His mother stood next to them. "There you are, Sleeping Beauty," she said as she gave Evette a hug.

Evette felt her face grow warm.

"Oh, now you know I'm just teasing you. Scoot on over here and take a look at my newest grandbaby."

The little one was pretty well hidden from view—decked out in a massive blanket and a tiny hat—but Evette thought he was adorable.

"He's so precious," she whispered.

"He is." Anthony stepped closer and put his arm around her.

Evette did her best to savor the priceless moment. This family was refreshingly tight-knit—much like her own.

"What did they name him?"

"Jacob Carson Edwards," said Mavis, beaming proudly.

After a few minutes Anthony yawned loudly. "I think it's time for me to get going. Are you ready to go?" he asked Evette.

"I sure am. Do you feel up to getting behind the wheel? Or should I drive?"

He chuckled. "That wouldn't do much good since I'd still have to drive after I dropped you off. I might as well wake up now."

The rest of the crowd began to disperse, and Evette joined in the round of hugs. "Tell Max and Stacy congratulations for me," she told Anthony's mother.

"I will, Honey. And don't be shy and stay away. Has Anthony invited you to one of our Sunday dinners yet?"

"I have, Mom," he answered. "But she hasn't been able to come yet."

"Well, don't be a stranger to us, Evette. We'd be glad to have you."

"I'd like to," she said. Evette had a feeling that even if she and Anthony remained nothing more than friends, his mother would still show her the same warmth.

"Before we leave, I want to find a cup of hot coffee somewhere," said Anthony. "Let's stop by the cafeteria on our way out.

Once they were in the car, Evette did her best to keep the conversation going because Anthony seemed suspiciously drowsy.

"Are you sure you don't want me to drive?"

"I'm sure. So quit asking," he said, laughing. He rolled down the window to let in some of the cool morning air. "Just keep talking to me."

"I'm glad I had the chance to meet your family."

"They were pretty excited to meet you too." He gave her a sideways glance. "They keep asking when we're getting married."

"And what did you tell them?"

"I told them I was waiting for you to make up your mind."

Evette's jaw dropped. "I can't believe you put all the blame on me. I mean—we've never even really discussed—at least, not seriously."

Anthony grinned sheepishly. "I guess I might have forgotten to tell you how I felt." He yawned again and fumbled for his Styrofoam coffee cup.

"You keep your eyes on the road," Evette said, handing him the hot drink. "We'll talk this over later. You're too sleepy to make any monumental decisions right now."

When they reached her house, he looked even more drowsy. "Are you sure you can drive?"

His reply was a gigantic yawn.

"Why don't you come inside and get a refill on that coffee? My mom usually has some going by now."

"Thanks," he said and followed her inside.

Her mother was up and about and, true to Evette's prediction, had brewed a large pot of coffee.

"Your dad went in early this morning," she said as she hugged Evette. "Did everything go well at the hospital?"

"Yes. The baby was born about an hour ago. It's a boy."

"Congratulations," her mother said to Anthony.

"Mom, I fell asleep at the hospital, but Anthony and the rest of his family pulled an all-nighter. I'm going to get ready for work, but could you make sure he looks sufficiently coherent before you let him get into his car?"

Her mother took a look at Anthony and ushered him to a chair at the kitchen table. "I'll do my best, but this boy needs some sleep."

"I know, but he insisted on driving."

Evette took another look at Anthony, who seemed unusually quiet.

"My goodness, he's asleep," said her mother. "You run and get ready, and I'll take care of him."

Evette was relieved to let her mother handle the job. While Anthony might insist to her that he could make the drive to his house, he would be less likely to disagree with one of his elders.

Half an hour later Evette bounded downstairs, refreshed, and ready to go to work. She peeked out the front window and saw Anthony's car still parked out front.

She found her mother in the kitchen, but no Anthony. "Where is he?"

"Shh." Her mother gestured toward the living room. "I made him lie down on the couch. He was too out of it to eat or drink anything, so I put my foot down and sent him in there. He should be okay to drive in a couple of hours."

Evette peeked in the room and watched him for several moments. Her mother had thrown a blanket over him, and his stocking feet hung over the armrest. He was out like a light and let out a few snores every once in awhile. *Cute,* Evette thought.

"Thanks for taking care of him, Mom. I hope you don't have anywhere to go."

Her mother shook her head. "Not really. I have to go grocery shopping, but that can wait until this afternoon. After he wakes up I'll do my vacuuming. I'm just glad he got you home all right."

"I am too. You should have seen me, talking nonstop about everything that popped into my head."

"Now are you sure you feel alert enough to make it to work?"

Evette waved her mother's concern away. "I spent the night in a hospital waiting room chair, but I'm okay—at least for the moment. I'll see you this evening."

❧

"Hey, how was the hospital?" Trevor wanted to know as soon as she reached the shop.

"Fine, I guess. I slept through most of it, believe it or not. But the baby's adorable. A little boy."

"Guess what?" said Drew. "Dad has determined that on a scale of one to ten Trevor's inventory skills are a minus two."

"Hey, I made a few innocent mistakes, and now he's in the back having a fit," Trevor defended himself.

"So what does that mean for the rest of us?" Evette asked.

"It means that we have to do inventory twice a month until he feels satisfied that things are being handled correctly. We have to work in teams of three; and you, Drew, and I are signed up for next weekend."

"No way." Evette's heart sank at the prospect. They usually did a full count of all products every other month. The job was extremely tedious—not to mention that being closed up in the storeroom for long periods of time was never fun.

She stared at Trevor. "You must have really messed up."

"Interesting how everyone's so quick to blame, but no one else volunteered to keep track of the day-to-day stock. It gets a little confusing, so cut me some slack."

Evette keyed in her code on the register and officially clocked in. "I can't do it this weekend. Anthony is taking me to the Muny to see a musical on Friday night."

"You have to unless Trevor wants to trade with you. He, Dad, and Justin are scheduled for the next go-around in two weeks," Craig explained.

Evette swallowed her pride and prepared to beg for mercy. "Come on, Trev—please switch with me. He bought these tickets three weeks ago. And they're doing my favorite musical."

Her brother smirked. "Ah, now look at how the tables have turned. Two minutes ago you were criticizing my job skills, and now you want me to show mercy so you can go sit outside and watch some play with your boyfriend."

Evette leaned on the counter. As much as she wanted to keep the date with Anthony, she didn't have much patience for Trevor's annoying foibles this morning. "Are you going to trade with me or not?"

"Yeah, I guess. It's not as if I have anything better to do."

"Thanks," she said.

"So I guess you and Anthony made it official?" asked Justin, stepping over to the counter.

Evette felt strange discussing her personal life with Justin. "Not really," she said. "We're still just friends," she said cautiously.

"Oh, come on—admit it," prodded Drew. "You two are not just friends. I mean, you spent the entire night with his family waiting for his nephew to be born."

"I would have come home, but I couldn't very well ask one of them to leave the hospital and take me home. They might have missed the big event."

"Yeah, likely story," Craig said, laughing.

Trevor singsonged under his breath, "Evette's got a boy-friend. Evette's got a boyfriend."

Craig and Drew chimed in and sang along while Justin stared at her.

Brothers. Evette shook her head, remembering how much fun she'd had with the women in Anthony's family. She loved her family, but on days like today she'd gladly trade one or more of the boys for a sister.

a&

The next week Anthony had to skip Wednesday night Bible study, but Evette went anyway. Since Justin had faithfully attended Sunday morning services with her, she invited him to come along, but he turned down the invitation.

"I like going on Sundays, but I'm not ready to give up another night of the week," he explained.

"I understand, and I'm not trying to force you to go," she told him. "Just thought I'd check and see."

"Thanks for the invite, but I'll stick to once a week for now."

Evette considered his words as she made the short drive to church. For the first few weeks Justin's interest in attending church and learning more about the Bible had been impressive.

But over the past few weeks his interest had waned drastically. He'd even skipped church altogether the previous week. A few of his buddies he'd met on the tour were in town, and he wanted to play a round of golf with them.

While she didn't approve of his choice, she didn't make an issue of it. As she'd had to do, Justin would have to make his own decision about how much he wanted to put into his relationship with the Lord. Evette no longer felt comfortable with the idea of missing church, but she also realized it had taken her years to make that decision.

On the one hand, she was sad that Justin didn't seem as excited about drawing closer to the Lord. She knew her own life felt dramatically different. The empty feeling had all but disappeared, and she woke up each day feeling more refreshed and relaxed than she remembered feeling since she was a little girl. From her discussion with Justin, Evette knew he still felt hurt and confused about his unsuccessful run at the pro tour, and she wished the same change for him.

On the other hand, knowing she and Justin didn't see eye-to-eye on spiritual issues made it easier to ignore the pangs of longing that sometimes resurfaced. While she couldn't deny that her feelings for Anthony grew stronger with each passing day, she still faced a jumble of emotions when it came to Justin. It was harder to walk away from her first love than she could have imagined. His name was embedded in so many of her memories of firsts—first date, first dance, first kiss, first proposal—the list went on and on.

On the other hand, he was also attached to some of her more forgettable firsts—first bout of jealousy (Jacquie Phillips had done everything in her power to get him to ask her to the senior prom); first mistrust (when he'd cheated on her during her sophomore year in college); and, of course, first broken engagement (no explanation needed).

Yet she still found herself wondering if she should give him a second chance. "What should I do, Lord? Which one is the right one for me?"

twelve

"What are your plans for next weekend?"

Evette shrugged. "I don't know. But the weekend after that is full. Remember our new inventory system at the store?"

Anthony nodded.

"Well, I was scheduled to work today and tomorrow; but since you'd already bought tickets for the play tonight, Trevor switched with me."

"I see. So how would you feel about going to Kansas City for a couple of days? We'd leave Friday morning and come back Sunday afternoon."

"We? I don't know—"

"Oh, it wouldn't be just you and me. Mom and Dad want me to drive them there to visit Max and Stacy. And Albert thinks he might come too." He cleared his throat. "I hope you didn't think I was suggesting anything—"

"Untoward, unseemly, improper," Evette supplied with a grin.

"Yeah. All of those."

She shook her head. "I know you weren't suggesting anything less than gentlemanly. I just thought I'd tease you a little."

"So will you come?"

"Let me think about it. Give me a few days to see if I can re-schedule my lessons and get someone to cover my hours at the store. I have to admit, a short road trip sounds like a great idea."

❧

The drive to Kansas City was perfect. Sunny weather and

extremely light traffic made the conditions ideal for a four-hour drive.

They rode in Albert's SUV in order to have more room for their weekend bags. Anthony and Albert sat in front, and Evette sat in back with Mavis and Claude, who were overjoyed at the prospect of seeing their grandbaby again.

As soon as they pulled into Max and Stacy's driveway, Max came out to greet them.

While the men took the bags inside, Evette helped Mavis carry in the baby gifts she'd brought.

Stacy was inside, making sandwiches. Mavis promptly told her to sit down. "Evette and I will do the cooking while we're here."

Stacy shook her head. "I can't let you do that. You are our guests."

Mavis stood her ground. "No, I won't have that. You sit down and enjoy that baby. If we lived closer, I'd let you cook. But since we don't get here that often, I insist on doing my share."

The sound of crying echoed over the house intercom. "I tried to put him down for a nap, but I think he must have realized he's missing out on some excitement," Stacy said. "I'll be right back."

While Stacy was gone, Mavis took inventory of the contents of the kitchen cabinets in order to plan meals for the next two days. If anything was missing, she had Evette take note of it and compile a grocery list. "And I plan to make at least a week's worth of casseroles while I'm here," she informed Evette.

Evette watched as the tiny dynamo of a woman put down stakes and took charge of the household. Within half an hour of their arrival she'd sent Stacy upstairs to nap while baby

Jacob slept and had shooed Claude and Max to the living room to assemble a baby swing. Albert was given the task of mowing the lawn, and Anthony was on the sidelines, waiting to be called into duty. "As soon as we finish this shopping list, Honey, you and Anthony can run to the store and get everything."

Evette nodded and continued to do as she was told. She couldn't help but wonder how Stacy felt when it came to Mavis's take-charge attitude.

After spending an hour in the kitchen with her, Evette decided that while Mavis definitely had a strong personality, she wasn't an overbearing mother-in-law type. She truly wanted to help out, but her manner wasn't mean spirited or condescending.

"Now," Mavis said, wiping her hands on a dishtowel, "please call everybody in here to eat lunch—except for Stacy. I'll fix her a plate and give it to her when the baby wakes up."

Evette called the men to the dining room and helped Mavis serve the sandwiches.

After lunch, Mavis sent everyone back to their jobs. While she started on her assembly line of casseroles, she had Evette accompany Anthony to the store.

"Double-check the list, and please don't forget anything," she cautioned as they headed to the car.

When they were well on their way to their destination, Anthony ventured a question. "So how did you enjoy your first hour under the tutelage of my mom?"

"It was—interesting," said Evette. "Actually I had fun."

"You didn't think she was being too bossy?"

She shrugged. "I don't think so. I think she's just trying to help."

Anthony laughed. "Tell that to Albert. He's still grouchy

that he had to cut the grass."

"I thought he didn't look so pleased."

"Yeah, that and the fact that Brienne had to work this weekend and couldn't come. Mom wouldn't let him back out because she said she needed an extra set of hands to help her out. He didn't realize it involved yard work."

"Poor Albert," said Evette.

"Poor Albert? What about Stacy? Mom ran the woman out of her own kitchen."

Evette shrugged. "She seemed pretty grateful for the break."

"You say that now," Anthony laughed.

"What's that supposed to mean?"

"It means, what if you and I were married and Mom came over and did that same thing in our house? Would you think it was nice then?"

The words "our house" filled Evette's imagination with a montage of warm images. She very much liked the idea of "our house" as long as Anthony was in the picture. "No, I don't think so. New babies are lots of work, and my mom always said she wished either set of our grandparents had lived closer when we were little."

Anthony seemed surprised. "So you wouldn't mind?"

Evette grinned. "As long as it didn't happen every day, I would welcome it. I think she's being really sweet."

"Well, I, for one, am glad you feel that way," said Anthony.

Evette sighed happily and looked out the window. There were no words to describe how it felt to fall in love.

&

"Ah, our traveler returns to the reality of daily life," Craig said as Evette entered the store Monday morning.

Evette closed her umbrella. "Can you believe that wind out there?" She peered out and focused on the dark gray sky.

"You know, I really dislike rainy, dreary days. Especially after the weather was so nice all weekend."

"How was the trip?" he asked.

"It was nice."

"Nice? That's all?"

Evette smiled. "I'll give you the condensed version. I spent the first day helping Anthony's mom cook. I think she made twelve casseroles. Saturday we went window shopping on the Plaza. Then we took a boat ride in Brush Creek—it's a waterway that runs along the outer border of the Plaza. Stacy's sister babysat Jacob, and Max took us all to dinner at the Cheesecake Factory. Sunday morning we went to church then returned to the house. I helped Mavis cook dinner, and then we got in the car and drove back."

"What time did you make it back here?"

"Around eight o'clock. I was exhausted and went straight to bed."

Craig sighed. "I think I need a vacation."

"Why don't you take some time off? With Justin around, it always feels like we're overstaffed."

"I think I will. Lisa wants to go to Chicago for the Fourth of July. I'll ask Dad if he can spare me for a few days."

Evette took a look at the daily schedule. "It looks as if you and I are the only ones working until noon."

"Yeah. And nobody's going to come in today with this kind of weather. We might even be able to close early. Justin had a lesson, but the man canceled because of the storm. I tried to call him, but there was no answer. I'm assuming he figured the lesson was off."

"So it's just you, me, and an empty store. What should we do?"

"Go home?" Craig joked. "No, I guess we can always

restock shelves. I'll run to the back and drag out some of the heavy boxes, and you stay out front in case someone ventures in."

"Will do," said Evette, as she took a seat behind the register. She found the remote to the television set and turned on the power. Normally her dad insisted it always be tuned to the Golf Channel, but in questionable weather they were allowed to switch to a local station to keep up-to-date.

The phone rang, and Evette answered. "Hello?"

"Evette?" It was Justin, but for some reason he sounded surprisingly unlike himself.

"Justin? Are you okay? You do know your student canceled his lesson, right?"

"I figured he would. I need a favor, though."

She sighed. "I don't know. Craig and I are the only ones here right now so I probably wouldn't be able to leave. Are you having car trouble again?"

"I guess you could say that. I wondered if you or one of your brothers could possibly pick me up and give me a ride home?"

"Where are you?" A flash of lightning tore through the horizon, followed by a gigantic clap of thunder. Evette shuddered. The one thing worse than a thunderstorm was being out in one. She surfed the channels to locate a station giving a weather report.

"At the hospital."

"What?" Evette's stomach turned, and she felt sick. "Did you say you were at the hospital?" Evette turned down the volume on the television and strained to listen to Justin. Why was he speaking so quietly?

"Yeah." He let out a shaky laugh.

"What happened? Are you okay?" Her words tumbled out in a rush. Evette anxiously glanced toward the storeroom door. What was keeping Craig so long?

"I had a car accident, and my car is totally undriveable."

"But what about you? Are you hurt?"

"Not too bad. I have some cuts and sprains—they said I don't have a concussion so there's no reason for me to stay overnight."

Another clap of thunder shook the building. Evette didn't like the idea of going out in the storm, but she hated to let Justin down. "Hold on a minute, and I'll see what we can do about getting you a ride home, okay?"

Evette ran back to the storeroom and hurriedly explained the situation to Craig. He picked up the extension and got the name of the hospital from Justin, then prepared to head out into the storm.

"Do you think he's okay?" Evette asked.

"I'm not sure. He sounds pretty out of it."

"Yeah, I noticed. Maybe they gave him some pretty strong meds."

Craig gave the interior of the shop a cursory glance. "I hate to leave you here by yourself. Do you want me to call Dad and ask him to come in?"

Evette shook her head. "I doubt anyone will come in now. I'll wait here until you get back."

Craig looked doubtful. "If you feel uncomfortable, lock up and go home, okay?"

Evette nodded dutifully. Craig was the perfect big brother. "I will."

"Be back as soon as I can," he said, tugging on his jacket and heading outside.

True to her prediction, no one ventured to the shop. The weather got worse, and Evette found herself pacing back and forth in front of the window. "Lord, please keep Justin and

Craig safe on the road."

Half an hour later Trevor arrived at the store, looking grim.

"Hey, you're not supposed to come in today," she said. "Just couldn't stay away?"

He lifted his eyebrows. "Hardly. I was sound asleep and got a call from Craig demanding I take your shift. He wants you to meet him at Mom and Dad's house."

Dread washed over Evette, and she was reluctant to voice her concerns, fearing what the answer would be. "Is something wrong with Justin?"

"Nothing serious, but he's in a lot of pain. When he talked to you on the phone, he wasn't being totally honest. Craig said the wreck knocked him around pretty good."

"So he took him to our house?"

"Yeah, and he wants you to go and help Mom take care of him."

"I see." Evette got her keys and purse. "I'll see you later."

On the way home she found herself worrying. Poor Justin. She was glad Craig had taken him to the house. He shouldn't have to be alone at a time like this.

At home her parents were busy upstairs, making Justin comfortable in Trevor's old room.

Justin seemed half asleep, but he opened his eyes when Evette came into the room. "How do you feel?" she asked, keeping her voice quiet.

"Not too good," he croaked.

She patted his hand and pulled up a chair next to the bed. "What can I do? Are you hungry?"

He shook his head. "No. . .just. . .sleepy."

Evette looked to her mother. "What did they give him?"

"I'm not sure, but he'll probably need more soon. He was complaining that his shoulder hurt a few minutes ago. Craig went to the pharmacy to get a prescription filled, and he should be back in a few minutes."

Her dad stood in the doorway. "I think we should let him rest for awhile. There's really nothing we can do."

Evette agreed. "Should I go back to the store then?"

Her dad shook his head. "I don't think that's necessary. I'll go. You stay here and help your mother with Justin."

After her dad left, Evette and her mother retreated to the family room. When Craig came, they gave Justin another dose of medicine, which promptly put him to sleep.

Evette and her mother took turns checking on him to make sure he was okay, but he slept most of the afternoon.

At six o'clock Evette took him a bowl of soup, and he insisted he wasn't hungry but asked for more medicine for his shoulder. Evette sat down next to the bed again. "You have to eat something before we give you anything for your shoulder."

She helped him sit up a little, then fed him several spoonfuls of soup. The medicine still made him groggy. While she fed him, he kept dozing off then awoke to ask her if he could go home.

Evette pressed her hand against his forehead to see if he might have a fever. It felt a bit warm, but she couldn't be certain since she didn't have a thermometer.

"Mom?" she called. "Could you come here for a minute?"

Moments later her mother entered the room. "What's wrong?"

"He feels a little warm. Do you think he could have a fever?"

Her mother felt his forehead and shrugged. "No, his temperature feels pretty normal to me. He just needs some food and rest."

Justin groaned. "Can I go home?"

"He keeps asking that," Evette said.

Her mother shooed Evette out of her seat and picked up the bowl of soup. "Justin, honey, you're going to have to work with me and eat this soup. The doctor told Craig that as long as you got rest and fluids, you would start feeling better soon. You can go home as soon as we think you're up to it."

Justin didn't argue any further but sat up and ate the soup. When he finished, he insisted on walking downstairs to sit in the family room with them.

"I don't think that's a good idea," Evette told him.

He leaned forward and covered his face with his hands. "Please let me go home."

Her mother rubbed his back softly. "Justin, as soon as I know for sure you can get around okay and you can cook for yourself, I'll let you go home. Until then you've got to do what I say so you can get better."

Justin didn't answer, but his shoulders shook as he made sniffling sounds.

Her mother leaned closer. "Now, Honey, why are you crying?"

He shook his head and mumbled something Evette couldn't decipher.

Her mother chuckled. "No, no, you're not being a burden. We want you to be okay, and I don't like the idea of your being home by yourself like this."

"Get me some tissues, Evette," her mother directed.

Evette found a box and handed it to her mother. Her mother passed the box to Justin for him to wipe his face.

Evette could hardly stand to watch this. In all the years she'd known Justin, she had never once seen him cry. Was he really that upset or had the medicine made him overly emotional? To see him in this condition was heartbreaking.

"Let's make a deal," her mother said. "If you want to come

downstairs, you have to eat another bowl of soup and drink two glasses of water. Can you do that for me?"

"Yeah," he said.

"All right then. Let's go." She and Evette helped him stand, but he wouldn't lean on either of them. He moved very slowly but finally made it to the bottom. Evette wondered if he would be able to make it back up later on.

Justin sat on the sofa. Her mother wasted no time giving orders. "I've got to check on this roast, and then I'll warm up some soup. You stay here, Evette, and keep him company."

Evette turned on the television and flipped to the sports channel. "Is this what you want to watch?"

Justin shrugged. They watched in silence until the golf highlights came on. At that point Justin started sobbing.

Evette gingerly hugged him, trying not to jostle his bruised muscles.

"Justin, please tell me what's wrong?"

He leaned on her shoulder. "I can't believe you guys are taking care of me after how I treated you. I feel so guilty."

"Don't feel bad," she said, trying to console him. "We forgive you. I forgive you."

"You do?"

"Of course."

"Thank you." He shifted in his seat to find a more comfortable position. Evette watched as he finally drifted off to sleep.

She quietly stood. He must have heard her because he opened his eyes briefly.

"Evette?"

"Yes?" she said, bracing for him to ask if he could go home.

"I love you." He closed his eyes and went back to sleep.

Unexpected tears sprang to her eyes. Blinking them away, she placed a light blanket over him and retreated to her room.

Feeling emotionally drained, Evette lay on her bed for several minutes. No matter how much she tried to convince herself that Justin's admission of love was medicine-induced, she couldn't forget his words.

Did he really still love her? Did she still love him?

Did I ever love him?

At that moment the phone rang. "Hello?"

"Hi, it's Anthony. I wanted to see how your day went."

"My day? It was—not too good." Evette tried to hold back the tears, but they wouldn't stop.

"Evette, calm down. Please tell me what's wrong."

She took a deep breath and gave him a detailed account of the day, starting with Justin's call from the hospital and ending with his "Evette, I love you."

"Oh, Evette, I'm sorry your day has been so difficult. Do you want me to come over?"

She shook her head, even though he couldn't see her. "No, that's okay."

"You know I'm not going to let you stay sad like this. What can I do to cheer you up?"

Evette smiled, hearing the concern in his voice. "Okay, tell me something happy. Some good news."

"Let's see—good news. My mom told me Stacy called to tell her that baby Jacob smiles whenever he hears the words 'Grandma' and 'Grandpa.' "

Evette chuckled, thankful for a reason to do so after such a trying day. "Is that so?"

"Yes. That's pretty amazing, considering he's not even three weeks old."

"Got any more good news?"

"Well, I had a call from a sports magazine asking me if I'd like to interview for a position."

Evette sat up straight. "An interview? Really?"

"Yeah." He sounded pretty pleased. "I've wanted to work for them for awhile."

"So if you get the job what does that mean? Will you keep working for the paper?"

"If I get the job I'll have to move to Boston, since that's where the main office is."

"Boston?" Evette tried to remember if Anthony had ever mentioned moving to Boston before today.

"Yeah, it's an in-house position."

"Oh." She tried to sound happy for him. "So when's the interview?"

"I'm flying there tomorrow."

"Wow, this is really fast. You know, I don't think you mentioned wanting to switch jobs before. Is this a new development in your life, or have I not been paying attention?"

"Both, I guess. I mean, I've been thinking about switching jobs, but I sent them my resume around six months ago. I never mentioned it because I assumed they weren't interested. But when I got home from work, out of the blue, they had left a message on my machine."

"Evette?" her mother called from downstairs.

"My mom's calling me. I think dinner's ready," she told Anthony.

"I'll let you go then. Would you pray for me tomorrow?"

Evette swallowed her disappointment. "Sure."

"I'll pray for Justin to feel better soon," he said. "I'm scheduled to arrive back in St. Louis around ten tomorrow evening. I'll probably call you Wednesday to let you know how it went."

After they finished talking, Evette didn't head downstairs immediately. She lay down again, this time deep in thought.

How could Anthony have neglected to tell her he wanted to move to Boston? Considering the fact that she felt pressure from him to make a decision about their relationship, this newest revelation didn't add up. How could he not realize a possible move to Boston might affect her decision?

Evette sighed in frustration. This reminded her of the day when Justin called to tell her he was going to stay on the tour full time. In his mind he had already broken up with her but didn't bother to inform her for several more months. *Once again I'm the last one to find out. Am I doomed to repeat the same scenario with different men?*

For once she didn't feel guilty that she hadn't been able to reach a decision about her relationship with Anthony. He might act more holy, but in the end he had turned out to be no different from Justin.

Justin might occasionally come across as annoying and immature, but he was not without redeeming qualities. And at least he apologized, she told herself as she headed downstairs.

Suddenly, the woozy, bruised, soup-eating man on the family room sofa seemed far more attractive and sincere than Anthony Edwards.

thirteen

The next day passed a bit more easily. Evette stayed home again to help her mother with Justin, but he improved rapidly. His aches and pains lessened considerably, and he only needed one dose of his medicine.

He still walked with a slight limp, but Evette had no doubt he would be feeling much more like normal by the end of the week.

Evette tried very hard not to think about Anthony's interview, but she was unsuccessful. Besides she had promised to pray that it went well.

After lunch, while Justin napped, Evette decided to find out what her mother thought of Anthony's news. She recounted her telephone conversation with him and waited for some feedback.

Her mother didn't answer right away but seemed deep in thought as she washed dishes.

"Mom?" Evette asked after a few minutes. "You didn't answer."

"I know." Her mother shrugged. "I'm not sure I have an answer. Have you prayed about this?"

Evette looked at the ceiling. "Yes. I've been praying for weeks about being Anthony's girlfriend, and I thought I had my answer—until this. He knows how I felt when Justin did the same thing, so how could he do the exact same thing?"

"Are you sure it's the exact same thing? You could be jumping to conclusions."

Evette bit her lip. "I don't think so. It's the same thing all over again. First he announces he's leaving, and then he'll want to break up."

Her mother chuckled. "How can you break up if you aren't dating?"

"Mom, you know what I mean. I'm speaking hypothetically here."

"Oh, I see."

Evette didn't miss the smile that spread across her mother's face. She plopped into a chair. "Mom, I know you think this is funny, but it isn't. I was this close to telling Anthony I was ready for the relationship. I even thought I loved him."

"Evette, Anthony and Justin are both good men. Neither one is perfect, but they both have their good qualities. But where Justin purposefully deceived you about his plans to be gone for longer than you had agreed, I don't see Anthony doing the same."

"You believe that whole story about his sending the resume ages ago and not thinking the magazine was interested?"

"I do. Anthony is a man of his word."

"But, Mom, we tell each other almost everything. If this was so important to him, why didn't he ever mention it? I could have prayed with him about it."

"I don't know. It's probably a personality thing. Some people count their chickens before they're hatched, and others don't. I see Anthony as the type to wait and see, especially if it concerns something that's really important to him. In case it didn't work out, he'd be able to cope with the disappointment without having too many people asking how he feels."

Evette shook her head. "I'm the exact opposite. If something big is about to happen to me, I want everybody to know about it so they can be happy for me or help me feel better if it doesn't pan out."

"I know you are," said her mother. "But I'm not like that. I like to keep things under my hat until I know it's going to work out."

"So you think I should assume that's where Anthony's coming from?"

"I think you should talk to him about it. That way you'll know for sure without having to rely on something we came up with ourselves."

"Okay, I guess I can do that. When he calls, I'll ask him about it."

&

Wednesday after work Anthony decided to call Evette. He still hadn't heard any news regarding the interview, but he wanted to touch base with her.

The phone rang several times, and Anthony was about to hang up when someone picked up the phone.

"Hello?"

He recognized the voice as Justin's. For a man who was supposed to be sick, he certainly sounded robust.

"Hi. Is Evette there?"

"Yeah, just a minute. Eve, telephone."

So now he was calling her Eve. Was that just a nickname or a term of endearment? Anthony tried not to let his imagination get carried away.

"Hello?"

"This is Anthony."

"I know. Justin told me," she explained.

"Oh. I thought I'd call and let you know how my interview went. It took you so long to answer the phone that I thought you might have gone to Bible study."

"No, I decided not to go tonight. Mom and I spent the day helping Justin get things going with the insurance company. It'll cost more than the car is worth to fix it so we're waiting to hear how much they'll pay. Then we had to pick up the rental car, collect the mail at his apartment, and take him to the doctor for a follow-up appointment. After all that, we were too tired to cook, so Dad took Mom out for dinner, and Justin and I stayed home and ordered a pizza. We were in the middle of a Monopoly game when you called."

"I hope he's feeling better."

"Oh, yeah. He's still got bruises and sore muscles, but he doesn't need those strong painkillers anymore. He has a limp from the sprained ankle, but he's feeling well enough to go to work tomorrow."

"That's great news."

"We're all relieved. It was such a shock seeing him in so much pain like that. Thanks for trying to cheer me up the other day. It really helped." She paused then continued talking. "Speaking of our conversation—tell me about your interview." Her voice seemed to have a false cheeriness, and he wondered what could be the matter.

"It was a pretty basic interview, I guess. They seemed to like my work, but I won't know anything until they give me a yes or a no. But thanks for praying—I really appreciate it."

"Anthony—could I ask you something?"

"Sure."

"About the interview—I'm a little curious to know why you didn't mention it before now."

"I told you I thought they weren't going to call. So there was no reason to bring it up."

"Oh." Her voice sounded flat.

"Why? Is there something wrong with that?"

"No—no, not really. I just—I mean, I thought we were pretty close, and we share so much with each other."

Anthony shrugged. "I'm sorry, Evette. Honestly, it never crossed my mind to tell you."

"But what if we'd been dating? Would you have told me then?"

"I don't know. Maybe. But I already said I didn't think they would respond. Does it really make that much of a difference?"

She was silent. Finally she said, "It would to me. I almost feel as if you were being dishonest with me. If I were your girlfriend, don't you think you should give me a heads-up if you're planning to move to Boston?"

Anthony now understood why she didn't seem enthusiastic about the interview. After considering her question for several seconds, he answered. "If we were a couple, then, yes, I would have mentioned the interview."

"Good."

"Good?"

"I mean, I'm glad you feel that way." She sighed. "Oh, Anthony, I'm sorry if I sounded—"

"As if you were interrogating me?"

"Okay, yes. But I'm just so cautious now, and the way you sprang that interview on me I couldn't help but wonder if you had done it on purpose."

"Why would I do something like that on purpose?"

"I don't know. But I couldn't figure out why you wouldn't tell me either, so I feared the worst. I was so scared to think you were planning to leave, as soon as I realized I was. . ." Her voice trailed off.

"Yes?" Anthony asked.

"Never mind."

"Let me guess," said Anthony. "Justin's in the room, hanging on every word you're saying."

"Yes."

Anthony laughed. "Are you busy Friday night? Maybe we can continue this conversation over dinner?"

"I wish I could, but it's my turn to do inventory, remember?"

"Can't you get one of your brothers to cover for you?"

"Sorry, but I don't think so. Trevor switched shifts with me last time, and I know for a fact he has a date Friday night. Plus I haven't even been to work this week because of everything that happened with Justin. I would feel bad if I tried to get out of inventory."

Anthony did his best to conceal his disappointment. "What about Saturday?"

"I promised Nina and Michelle I'd go to the symphony."

"Sunday?"

"Sunday is good. After church?"

"Yes, I'll take you out to dinner."

"I'm looking forward to it," she said. "Talk to you later."

❧

"That's it," Justin said, closing the ledger they used for inventory records.

Evette placed a hand to her forehead and crumpled dramatically to the floor.

Justin laughed and leaned against the wall.

"Boy, am I glad that's done. I can't believe we finished so quickly."

Evette smiled. "Thanks to another thunderstorm, we spent all day cooped up back here. But I guess it's worth it since we finished early." *But if I had known this was going to happen, I'd have accepted Anthony's invitation to dinner tonight. It's not even eight o'clock yet.*

Justin glanced at his watch. "You know, it's still kind of early. Want to see a movie?"

Evette yawned. "I don't know. Do you have one in mind?"

Justin reached down to help her up. "Why don't we ride over to the cinema and see what's playing? If nothing looks good, we can at least get some frozen custard."

Evette blew out a sigh. "I'm a little tired, but, after being in the storeroom for so long, going out might do me more good than heading straight home." She gave him a close look. "But the real question is, how do you feel? I don't want you getting worn out."

He waved away her concern. "I'm fine. Didn't you notice the limp is almost gone?"

"I did. You are a totally different man from four days ago." He was almost a hundred percent again. Yesterday after work he had convinced Evette's mother that he was doing well enough to go back to his own apartment. It was good to see him back on his feet again. At the rate he was recovering, he would probably be able to resume teaching on Monday.

"So are we going?" he asked.

"Yes. I'm ready whenever you are." She followed him out into the shop. Her dad and Craig were preparing to close up.

"You two going somewhere?" her dad wanted to know.

"We're going to get some fresh air," Evette announced. "And we may see a movie or just go for ice cream."

"Who's driving?" asked Craig.

"I will," Evette answered. The issue of Justin's tendency to drive too fast had caused her brothers some concern. Although they were happy he wasn't seriously injured, none of them felt comfortable riding as a passenger if he drove.

"How will I get home?" Justin wanted to know.

"I'll bring you back here so you can pick up your rental car," Evette explained.

"Have fun and be careful," her dad called after them.

The multiplex theater was crowded, typical of a Friday night. After much discussion they decided to watch a new animated movie. At first Justin protested. "It's a kiddie film," he pointed out.

"I know, but I've been wanting to see this one. Please?" Evette asked.

"Fine," Justin gave in grudgingly. Evette offered to buy the tickets, but Justin refused. After he paid at the box office he said, "Why don't you go in and find seats, and I'll get some snacks."

"Okay. Do you still like to sit in the middle of the theater?"

"Yes. And do you still like buttered popcorn and cherry licorice?"

"I sure do." Evette hurried inside to find a good place to sit while Justin headed toward the concessions area.

The theater was full of families, and little kids ran around, laughing and even screaming at random intervals. The ratio of youngsters to adults was probably four to one, and many of the grown-ups wore harried expressions.

Miraculously she found a middle seat with ease. The families seemed clustered close to the aisle seats. Evette figured they wanted to have easy access for the endless rest room trips children were notorious for.

After settling in, Evette surveyed the room once more. The kids were definitely enjoying themselves. She smiled, wondering how it must feel to be free to run around and laugh with abandon, not caring what anybody else thought.

"Evette?" A familiar voice pulled her from her thoughts.

She turned and found Anthony looking down at her.

"This is a coincidence. I didn't know you were into animated films," he said. "And I thought you were doing inventory this evening."

"Well, we finished early, and a cartoon seemed like a welcome change after spending all day counting and recounting things."

"Uncle Anthony? I need to go to the bathroom!" A little boy tugged at Anthony's sleeve. An even smaller toddler hugged Anthony's leg.

He smiled at Evette. "These are my nephews, Miles and Dennis. They're Latrice and Donald's boys," he said then looked down at his nephew. "Hold on just a minute, okay? Can you do that?"

The boy nodded. Anthony gestured to several seats in the row where Evette sat. "Are those taken?"

"I don't think so."

"Would you mind holding three for us?"

Evette nodded. "Sure, no problem."

As she watched Anthony hurry back down the stairs with the two boys in tow, she realized she'd forgotten to mention she hadn't come alone. *Surely he doesn't think I decided to come by myself—but he probably doesn't expect to see Justin here either.*

While she mulled over these thoughts, Justin returned. "The line out there is so long that I thought I'd miss the first part of the movie," he said.

First things first, she decided. *Might as well tell Justin what's going on.* "Guess who else is here?" she said brightly.

"I have no idea. And here is your candy," he said, handing her the package.

"Anthony Edwards."

Justin didn't say anything but sighed loudly.

Evette pretended not to notice his disappointment. "He's here with two of his nephews."

"Oh." Justin glanced over the crowd. "I don't see him."

She cleared her throat. "He had to leave for a few minutes, but I'm holding their seats." She glanced at the empty seats at Justin's side.

Justin eyed the chairs then gave her an exasperated look. "You're kidding me."

"No. I should have asked, but he was in a hurry—one of the kids needed to run to the rest room, and I couldn't tell him not to sit here, could I?"

"You could have at least told him you were on a date."

"A date?" Evette was flabbergasted. "You never said anything about a date."

Justin didn't seem to hear her question but went on with his complaint. "Why does that guy turn up like a bad penny every time you and I get a few minutes together?"

Evette stifled a laugh. "A bad penny?" she repeated. "I haven't heard that in years."

"I'm serious, Evette. I know we've had our disagreements and misunderstandings in the past, but I thought we were making strides. I thought maybe you might be ready to take me back." He leaned closer. "Don't you remember what I said the other day?" He lowered his voice to a whisper. "I still love you."

Evette spotted Anthony and the boys coming back and quickly shushed Justin. "We can discuss this later."

Anthony eyed Justin and gave Evette a questioning glance. "I guess we had a misunderstanding. I didn't realize you weren't here alone. Should we sit somewhere else?"

Justin merely shrugged, but Evette reassured Anthony the original seating arrangement was fine. Besides the theater was nearly full.

Justin must have felt apologetic, because he waved Anthony and the boys into the row. "Come on—don't worry about it."

As soon as Anthony had his nephews settled, the lights dimmed, and the movie began. Evette didn't know what to do. She could feel both Justin and Anthony staring at her from time to time. The tension didn't ease but grew worse.

At one point Justin leaned over and quite conspicuously put his arm around her shoulders.

Before she could wiggle away, one of Anthony's nephews exclaimed, "Eww—Uncle Anthony, are they gonna kiss?"

Justin quickly removed his arm, Anthony gave her a disapproving glance, and Evette stifled a laugh. The situation wasn't all that funny, but she'd rather laugh than cry. Several people turned around to see what the fuss was about, and Evette wanted to melt into the floor.

The only truly horrible part about this was that she still had to make Anthony understand that she and Justin weren't dating and tonight hadn't been planned. She didn't want him to think she and Justin were sneaking around behind his back.

From the look on his face the resolution was easier said than done.

The film turned out to be rather cute, but by the time it ended Evette wanted nothing more than to go home. Fast. She very much doubted that now would be a good time to try to sort things out with Anthony.

As soon as the house lights flickered on, Evette said good-bye to Anthony and his nephews then ushered Justin outside.

The situation had grown so awkward that staying to chat and going home rated the same on the discomfort scale. She would call Anthony in the morning to explain, and she would set Justin straight on the way back to the store.

"Can you tell me what just happened in there?" Justin

asked once they were on the road. "Can you tell me why you invited him and two little kids to be a part of our date?"

"It's not a date. We never agreed to date, Justin. But you know that. You ended the relationship, and I want to keep it that way," she answered.

"Are you sure? Have you even taken time to think it over?"

Evette nodded. "Positive. In fact I've probably spent too much time thinking it over. I like our friendship the way it is, but we are not anywhere near being a couple again."

"Can you at least give me a reason?"

"I can give you a lot of reasons. One, I have a hard time trusting a man who promised to marry me and called it off without any regard for how I felt. Two, I don't think we're on the same spiritual level, and I refuse to get involved with a man who isn't serious about his relationship with the Lord. Three, I'm not attracted to you anymore. Four—"

"You know what—I don't think I want to hear any more." Justin shook his head. "But I think you're just acting out of fear. A lot about me has changed, and you haven't stopped to notice."

Evette sighed. "Yes, you have changed. And I like the new Justin a lot better. But I'm in love with Anthony."

He nodded, looking straight ahead. "I guess I knew that already. I saw it that day I got back and he was at your house eating ice cream."

"I think I knew it then too." She chose her next words carefully. "And I'm sorry if my indecision made you feel—"

"As if I had a chance?"

Evette nodded.

"Don't feel too bad about it. We all make mistakes. I guess I deserve this for what I did to you."

"Don't say that, Justin. It doesn't help either of us to keep dredging up the engagement. It's over, but we still get along. I think that's something of a miracle in itself, wouldn't you say?"

"It is. And I'm happy for you, Eve. You deserve to be happy. I just wish something good would happen for me."

"I'll pray for you to meet the right woman, Justin. I know God will lead you to her."

"Thanks, Evette."

"You're welcome." She remembered Michelle's and Nina's questions about Justin a few weeks ago. "By the way, did I ever mention the float trip my Sunday school class is taking?"

fourteen

Anthony awoke to the sounds of loud cartoons and little-kid exclamations. He rolled over and put the pillow over his head. After all the trouble he'd had falling asleep the night before, being awakened at seven o'clock was not appealing.

After several minutes of continued cacophony, he shuffled down the hallway to check on the boys. He held on to the hope that he could convince them to sleep for another hour or so, but that option would only work if they were moderately still and quiet.

To his dismay the boys were not only awake but having an acrobatics competition on the fold-out bed.

Rubbing the sleep out of his eyes, he cleared his throat. "Hey, hey, calm down. Didn't Uncle Albert tell you to stop doing flips on this bed last night?"

The two boys nodded and sat down. They appeared duly chastened, and Anthony felt a bit more compassion. His nephews loved spending weekends with him and Albert. The last thing he wanted was to nit-pick over every little thing they did and take the fun out of it for them. It would take away from the adventure of being away from home for a couple of days.

Anthony remembered well the many scrapes he and Albert had managed to get into when they were young. He also recalled the countless numbers of times their mother had spent chasing them around the house warning them to be careful. He could hear her voice in his head even now: "Watch the lamp! Don't run on the stairs! If you break that vase—! Don't play so rough!"

Anthony located the remote control and adjusted the volume to a more tolerable level. As much as he hated being the bad guy, it was time for a talk.

"Look, fellas—I don't want to keep repeating the same things over and over. I want you guys to have fun. But we have to play safe. No flips or wrestling allowed without me or Albert supervising, okay?"

The pair nodded solemnly.

"Besides, if somebody got hurt, your mommy would be upset with me and Albert. Then she wouldn't let you sleep over anymore, and that wouldn't be any fun, right?"

Again they nodded. "Uncle Anthony, can we play video games?" asked Miles.

Anthony yawned and glanced down the hall toward Albert's room. The door was shut, and he felt a twinge of jealousy that his brother still slept peacefully.

Mornings like this helped him to be grateful he didn't have kids of his own yet. He liked the idea of having a family and often yearned for a wife and kids. But sometimes these early Saturday mornings and the responsibility of two little boys made fatherhood seem a bit less exciting.

He had strict orders from Latrice to make certain the boys played kid-appropriate games. That meant nothing that involved car crashes or fighting. Instead it meant educational games that helped the boys learn something, like adding or learning new words. And their play had to be supervised. After one hour of video games they had to switch to another activity. "Because I don't want my kids sitting in front of the TV all day," she said.

The list went on and on. Anthony didn't feel up to the task right now.

He scratched his chin and yawned again. Maybe he could change the subject. "Don't you want to watch some of these good cartoons?"

Dennis shook his head. "No, let's play the games now. I saw this cartoon yesterday."

Anthony sighed. It appeared they wouldn't be easily swayed. He cast one more longing look toward his room and sighed again at the thought of his pillow.

He stood up. "Okay. Let me make some coffee, and then we'll play the game."

"Yeah!" The boys, apparently having forgotten his mini-lecture, jumped up and down on the bed. Alarmed at the dangerously creaky noises the sofa sleeper was making under the stress of two jumping boys, Anthony hurriedly got them to sit down and watch television until he returned from the kitchen.

"Remember—no flips, jumps, or wrestling," Anthony called over his shoulder.

Anthony decided to forgo the trouble of the coffeemaker and settle for instant. The sooner he made it back to the family room, the less of a chance there was the boys would get restless and find some new way to break one of Latrice's rules.

Anthony added an extra teaspoon of crystals to the water and put the mug into the microwave.

"Uncle Anthony? I'm hungry." Dennis leaned against the doorway. "Can I have a doughnut?"

"Well, how about some cereal?" Latrice also forbade excessive consumption of doughnuts. Although he and Albert always kept a stash of them in the house, he didn't want to give the boys too much sugar. Especially since they already seemed pretty energetic this morning. They'd had that candy at the show, and then Albert brought out the gummy worms late last night.

"Aww, I don't want cereal!" He stamped his pajama-covered foot on the floor.

Uh-oh. This kind of whining was also on Latrice's list of no-nos. But it also signaled that certain little ones needed a nap. Anthony picked up Dennis and carried him back to the living room. If he could get them both back to bed, maybe he could catch a few extra winks. "No cereal? But I have that colorful kind you like."

"I want some cereal," Miles chimed in.

"I'm sleepy," said Dennis.

That makes two of us, Anthony thought.

He put Dennis on the bed, and the little boy crawled under the covers without any protest.

Miles watched his brother and let out a yawn. "I'm not tired," he announced.

"You aren't?"

Miles shook his head. "You said we could play the game."

"But we can't play without Dennis. We have to wait for him to wake up."

Miles put out a hand to shake his brother. "Wake up. Uncle Anthony said so."

"Leave me alone," Dennis whined. "Uncle Anthony, he hit me."

"Let him rest," Anthony told Miles. He chuckled and patted Dennis's head. "That's okay. You can go back to sleep. We'll wait for you."

Miles yawned again, this time a bit louder.

Anthony turned the TV off and pulled back the covers. "Why don't you lie down while your brother takes his nap?"

The boy protested, even as he snuggled under the blanket.

"But I'm not tired."

"I know you're not. You don't have to go to sleep. Just lie here until Dennis wakes up."

"For how long?"

"I don't know. He'll wake up when he's not tired. And no pinching or pushing. Let him sleep, okay?"

"Okay."

Anthony could tell by Miles's constant and prolonged blinking that the boy was quickly headed toward dreamland.

With a sigh of bliss Anthony tiptoed back to his room. As he lay down, he prayed the boys would sleep for at least three hours.

The moment he was comfortable, the phone rang. Sitting up, he groaned and reached for the receiver. He fervently hoped the caller wasn't Latrice or Donald, wanting to say hello to the boys. They seemed to call at the most inopportune times—like now—just as he'd coaxed Miles and Dennis back to sleep.

"Hello?"

"Anthony? It's Evette."

Anthony took a deep breath. The vision of Justin with his arm around Evette had kept him awake last night much longer than he liked to admit. He had tried his best to remain patient while she made her decision about their relationship, but now he wondered if she weren't trying to hold onto him while she decided if she wanted to take Justin back. The last thing he wanted to be was someone's safety date.

Careful to keep his emotions in check, he answered. "Hi, Evette."

"You sound a little groggy. Did I wake you?"

"Not really. My nephews kept me up late and got up early, so I'm a little incoherent at the moment."

"I guess you know I'm calling about last night, but if this is a bad time I can wait a few more hours."

He shook his head. "No, I'm fine." He paused to give her the opportunity to speak first.

"I know this sounds cliché, but what you saw last night wasn't the way it is. Justin and I are officially friends."

"So are you and I, but that hasn't stopped us from developing deeper feelings for each other."

"I know—I know." She sounded tired, and Anthony wondered if her night had been as sleepless as his own. "I admit I was a little—confused. I do have feelings for you, and I was struggling with leftover feelings for Justin."

Hearing her admit it hurt far worse than the suspicion she felt that way. What did she want from him? Love? Plain old friendship?

Anthony didn't think he could deal with this roller coaster she seemed bent on putting him through. One day he felt certain that she loved him, and the next she seemed to lean more in the direction of reconciling with the man who had mercilessly broken her heart.

Anthony rubbed his forehead. Could this get any more confusing?

"Are you still there?" Evette asked.

"I'm still here. I've been thinking, and maybe we both messed up somehow. When I signed up to take those lessons, I asked you to come back to church. I had two reasons for doing so. I wanted to see you more often, but I also wanted to draw you back to the church family. I knew you had drifted away, and I felt it was only a matter of time until you quit coming completely."

"And you were right," she said. "I felt out of touch. I probably would have started finding excuses not to go to church at all. So I'm glad you did what you did."

Was that the sole reason You brought me into her life, Lord? Was it careless of me to let my emotions progress beyond friendship?

"And maybe that was all I was supposed to do," he told her. "Albert warned me from the beginning to examine my priorities. He suspected I had ulterior motives, and I did."

"But I—"

"No, Evette. I have something else to tell you. The magazine called yesterday afternoon. They filled the position I wanted, but they have a temporary opening. They want me to come for a month, and they've indicated they might be able to hire me permanently if things go well."

"Oh." Her voice was flat. This wasn't the way he'd planned to break the news, but perhaps this was better. Not being able to see her face made things slightly less difficult.

"Are—are you going?"

"I think so. I'm not that happy about leaving St. Louis, but if I'm going to go this is an ideal way. I get to test the waters for a month, and if I don't like it, I can come back."

"What about your job?"

"I'm taking two vacation weeks and two unpaid weeks."

"Your apartment?"

He chuckled. "Albert's willing to live alone for a month."

"And—us?"

"I'm not sure there is an 'us.' I know we've both been praying, and I think this job opening is part of the answer. It wouldn't make any sense to start a relationship just before I move to Boston. We'd both be miserable."

"We would."

"I should be back the first week in August—I hope in time for the float trip." Anthony hated to change the subject, but it didn't make sense to get his hopes up and have them repeatedly dashed by the cold hard facts. Evette was still in love with Justin.

Evette cleared her throat. "Well, I apologize again for waking you so early. When do you leave?"

"Monday morning."

"So you'll be at church."

"Of course. But I think I'll need to cancel our dinner. I'll probably be running around, tying up loose ends, packing, and things like that."

"Oh, of course. I'll pray for you while you're gone. I hope the job turns out to be everything you expected and more."

"Thanks, Evette. I can use the prayer support."

"Anthony?" she asked. "Before we hang up, I want to say thanks."

"You're welcome. But why are you thanking me?"

"Oh, for lots of reasons. But mostly because you reached out to me when I needed that extra push to get things straight with the Lord. I respect you deeply for that."

The thank-you was bittersweet for Anthony. He didn't feel he had done the wrong thing by asking Evette to spend more time with her church family, but she must have agreed to consider a romantic relationship only because she had somehow felt indebted to him.

Anthony shook his head. It wasn't supposed to turn out this way. Even as he tried to think of something to say, another frustration surfaced. He couldn't help feeling that the extra "push" she referred to had helped pave the way for her reconciliation with Justin.

There was no way to deny how he felt about that situation. Jealous. He wanted so much to tell her how much he loved her and beg her to stay away from Justin, but he was too late.

Obviously this thank-you from Evette had two meanings. She did feel some amount of gratitude for how he had challenged her to get involved at church again. But she was also thanking him for letting her off the hook about the relationship.

"Evette, you don't have to thank me. I just tried to do what I felt the Lord was leading me to do. I didn't get everything right, but I'm glad my mistakes didn't send you running away."

"I wouldn't run from you," she said.

Anthony was so close to blurting out how he felt that it took every ounce of his self-control to say good-bye and hang up the phone.

This was the way it had to be. Anthony lay down and tried to catch a few more winks. As tired as he felt, though, he couldn't relax enough to fall asleep.

He finally got up and started sorting out piles of clothes to take to Boston. As he worked, he vowed never to engage in a crusade to "help" any other beautiful women grow closer to the Lord.

fifteen

Sunday morning Justin arrived at Evette's house just before she left for Sunday school.

"Do you mind if I ride with you?" he wanted to know.

"Of course not."

"And don't worry—I won't mistake this for a date. I did some thinking yesterday, and I'm okay with the friendship."

Evette laughed. "I'm glad we finally see eye-to-eye on this."

"Me too."

That morning, at the end of the service, Justin surprised Evette and her whole family by walking down to the altar and announcing he wanted to rededicate his life to the Lord.

The happiness she felt from this news was shadowed by the fact that she didn't get a chance to say good-bye to Anthony. He was completely surrounded by so many others who wanted to say good-bye that Evette finally gave up. Her family and Justin wanted to go out to dinner, and she didn't want to keep them waiting.

Maybe she could call or e-mail him while he was away. As much as it stung to know he preferred Boston to a relationship with her, she hoped their friendship wouldn't come to an abrupt end.

≈

"Have you heard whether or not Anthony's going to make it back for the float trip?"

Evette wished Nina and Michelle would stop asking her questions about Anthony. In the twenty-eight days since he'd left, she had received only one brief E-mail from him and nothing else. If she'd heard any more news it was because his mother or one of his sisters gave her an update.

Picking at her Caesar salad, Evette shrugged. "I have no idea."

"If he does, we'll have an even number of canoes," said Nina. "I saw the sign-up sheet Sunday."

"So what are you packing?" asked Michelle.

"I suggest you bring clothes you don't care about getting wet and muddy. It's a camping trip, not a fashion show," said Nina.

"I still can't believe you two talked me into this," Evette said. "I don't camp. I don't paddle canoes."

"If you stayed home, you'd be sitting around wondering how much fun you were missing. So try to be at least a little excited about it, okay?"

"Besides," added Nina, "the campout is only for one night. It'll be over before you know it."

"I guess so," Evette admitted. "And the more I think about it now, the more I'm starting to get used to the idea. At least I'll get to take a day off from work. That's always fun."

"That's the spirit," Nina said, smiling. "Hey, does anyone want to share a piece of cake with me? I think the waiter's coming back in a few minutes."

"I'm not that hungry," said Evette.

Michelle gave them a mournful look. "I want the cake, but I'm on a diet. Maybe another day. Oh, girls, guess what?" Michelle said in a conspiratorial tone. "Yesterday Justin stopped by my house and left a bouquet of daisies on my doorstep. Isn't that sweet?"

Evette smiled indulgently. Justin had wasted no time getting better acquainted with Michelle, and as happy as she was for them, it sometimes felt a little strange to hear another woman gushing over the man who would have been her husband.

"You know," Nina said, sounding wistful, "Todd never brings me flowers anymore. He did all the time when we first started dating, but that wore off pretty fast."

"Already?" said Michelle. "You've only been dating for two months."

"No kidding. But he's a sweetie, so I think I'll keep him—despite his lack of floral gifts."

"This has been so much fun, but I need to get back to work," said Evette. "Plus I still need to shop for some of the items from the things-to-pack list we got last week for the trip."

"I need to do that too," said Michelle.

Nina signaled the waiter to bring their checks. "I guess you two have spared me from ordering that cake."

"That's what friends are for," Michelle said, laughing.

Evette paid her portion of the bill and hurried out to the parking lot. She had to teach a lesson in forty-five minutes and wanted to be certain she arrived on time.

As she drove, she analyzed her emotions. For better or for worse, she had changed since Anthony's departure.

Before he'd left, she had been trying to learn what it meant to be whole in Christ, and still she had somehow missed the mark. While she struggled with the desire to have a significant other, she'd also felt secure in the fact that for a time both Anthony and Justin had been waiting in the wings.

She had gone to church, started a daily quiet time again, and began studying the Bible. But she hadn't been completely honest with herself. That empty feeling still lurked beneath the surface, and after Anthony left and Justin started dating Michelle, it had come back with a vengeance.

Evette had moped around for an entire week, not really

bothering to open her Bible. Instead she searched for some kind of balm to soothe her hurts.

She bought chocolate, went shopping, watched funny movies, and cried herself to sleep at night. That hole had grown so large that she sometimes wondered if it would overtake her and transform her into an empty shell of a person.

Finally, one night, as she lay restlessly trying to fall asleep, she remembered Gene's lesson on being whole. Feeling discouraged, she got up and located her Bible. This time she read a bit further in order to gain a better understanding of the passage.

" 'Love the Lord your God with all your heart and with all your soul and with all your mind.' This is the first and greatest commandment. And the second is like it: 'Love your neighbor as yourself.' All the Law and the Prophets hang on these two commandments."

Evette couldn't stop the tears from running down her face. She got down on her knees and asked the Lord to show her how to give every part of her life to Him.

"I want to be whole. And I feel such a void now that Anthony and Justin are gone—I know I'm not supposed to feel this way, but I do. Please show me how to do this correctly."

"Love your neighbor as yourself." The same five words played again and again in her memory.

Do I love my neighbor as myself? After some thought she determined she hadn't been very honest with either Justin or Anthony. She had kept them both within arm's reach until she was certain of her decision.

And now she had neither of them. Yet, if she had been in their shoes, she would have been offended that she hadn't been completely honest about how she felt about them both.

She prayed again. "Lord, I messed up on this part about

loving my neighbor as myself. Please forgive me. I want to do better at this. I give it all to You. Everything. The empty feeling, the pain, the confusion—all of it. I'll let You handle it from now on."

Evette stayed on her knees for awhile longer. By the time she finally crawled back into bed, she felt drained but free. So many things that had been bothering her were out of her hands and no longer troublesome.

This new feeling reminded her of how she felt when there was heavy lifting to be done at the store. She didn't pace around the box or fret and frown about how she should handle it. She didn't devise some plan to move it; instead she called her dad or brothers for help. Sometimes they wouldn't get to it right away, but she never took that to mean they wouldn't ever move it. She gave them complete control and knew in her heart it would be done.

She had asked Jesus to make her whole again, and she knew He would.

As her heavenly Father, God loved her even more than her earthly father did.

And, even though she might not understand the process, Evette was determined to let the Lord guide her life completely.

The pastor had preached from Isaiah 55 the previous Sunday. Remembering the Scripture passage, Evette found it appropriate for the change that had taken place in her life: "For my thoughts are not your thoughts, neither are your ways my ways. . .so is my word that goes out from my mouth: it will not return to me empty, but will accomplish what I desire and achieve the purpose for which I sent it."

Since then Evette felt more secure than she ever had. She missed Anthony, but God would take away that void— because His words didn't return to Him empty.

✌

"I can't believe how hot it is this early in the morning," Evette said as she and Justin pulled into the church parking lot the morning of the float trip. "I'm beginning to think that if the boat overturns it wouldn't feel half bad."

"No kidding." He laughed.

Several of the others had already assembled and were loading their bags onto the church bus.

"Do you know how long of a drive it is to the river?" Justin asked.

"I heard it's three or four hours," she said.

Justin lifted his eyebrows. "I hope they fixed the bus's air conditioning."

"Me too," she agreed. A couple of weeks earlier the singles' group had taken the bus downtown to a baseball game and discovered the AC was broken. Although the ride to the stadium was only a little over half an hour, it had still proved quite uncomfortable.

Justin carried both his and Evette's bags as they made their way to the rest of the group.

Nina spotted them and waved. "Evette, I can't believe you actually came. I told Michelle I suspected you would try to skip out on us."

"Ha, ha, very funny," she joked.

"Not too funny, though. She looked pretty hesitant when I picked her up," said Justin. "I kind of figured she was going to find a reason to make me take her back home, but she didn't."

"Well, don't count your chickens before they're hatched." Evette chuckled. "I'm not on the bus yet."

Michelle waved to someone behind Evette. "Well, look who made it back," she said. "You are just in time."

Evette turned around and saw Anthony walking toward

them. Two days ago she had seen Dana at the grocery store, and his sister reported that Anthony might not get in until Saturday evening—too late for the float trip.

Immediately he was surrounded by people saying hello and inquiring how his month in Boston had gone.

Evette hung back until the crowd dispersed a bit. As soon as he could, he came over and joined the little group where she, Nina, Michelle, and Justin waited.

The first few minutes were filled with meaningless small talk, mostly about the weather. Since it was so hot, everyone had something to contribute to the conversation, and there were no awkward silences.

Evette felt him watching her from time to time as they talked. She wondered what he was thinking. Had he decided to move to Boston for good?

"I think we should get on the bus," Michelle suggested.

"Right now?" said Nina. "Girl, that bus has been closed for at least a week. I am not stepping into that oven until it's time to leave."

"You know I have to sit in the front, or I'll get carsick," Michelle protested.

"I'll get on the bus with you," said Justin.

The rest of the group seemed to have the same idea, and within minutes everyone started piling inside. Michelle and Justin claimed the seat closest to the front, and Nina and Evette sat behind them.

"Girl, I cannot believe Todd had to work this weekend," Nina said, shaking her head. "He never seemed that excited about coming anyway. I think he signed up for overtime on purpose."

"Maybe," Evette answered, but she didn't pay much attention as Nina continued talking. Anthony sat down in the seat across from them, and, for the moment, he was alone.

He made eye contact with her and smiled. The old butterflies returned. Had he changed his mind about a relationship?

Evette was curious, but the thought didn't consume her, nor did the old void rear its ugly head. She had placed all of this in the Lord's hands, and she wasn't about to try to take it back. Her life was far less complicated without it.

Just before the bus departed, one more car pulled into the parking lot, and a man jumped out, waving his hands.

"Looks as if we have one more," said the driver.

Kaycee, the trip coordinator, checked her roster. "Really? I thought we were all accounted for. Who could we be missing?"

Their questions were answered when Todd boarded the bus.

He flashed a smile at Nina. "I switched shifts at the last minute with someone else."

The bus was almost completely full, and he looked around for a seat.

"I have an empty space here," Anthony said, waving him over.

"Thanks, Man." He sat down as the bus rumbled to a start. Looking across the aisle at Nina, he asked, "Are you surprised?"

"I'm shocked. But I'm happy too," she said.

Evette glanced across the aisle, and Anthony smiled. She returned the smile and watched as Nina and Todd conversed back and forth. Shaking her head, she wondered why those two didn't just sit together since they were talking only to each other.

After an hour on the road Anthony dozed off, and Evette felt a bit drowsy herself. Since she had no one to talk to, she leaned against the window and decided to get some rest.

She woke up as they arrived at the campground. The plan

was to set up camp as quickly as possible then drive over to the river and begin the four-hour float trip.

Evette helped Nina and Michelle set up their tent, and they teased her mercilessly when she did a thorough spider check.

"Girl, if a spider wants to get in here, I doubt you can keep him out." Nina laughed.

"Yeah? Well, you can say whatever you want, but I bet you wouldn't be thrilled to wake up in the middle of the night to find some eight-legged creature had taken up residence in your sleeping bag, would you?"

Michelle shook her head. "Come on, Evette. We need to get back on the bus. I brought my strongest flashlight, and we'll do another bug check before we turn in tonight."

ಶ

"Haven't had much rain this year, you know," the man at the boat rental was telling Kaycee. "River's pretty low in places, but that shouldn't affect the trip. And you don't have to worry about rapids or anything."

Anthony scanned the crowd for Evette. Since Michelle and Justin and Nina and Todd seemed to be paired together, there was a chance Evette didn't have a canoe partner.

He saw her standing near the bus, spraying her arms and legs with insect repellent. He waved to get her attention and jogged over to talk to her.

"Do you have an empty spot in your canoe?"

She chuckled. "I guess I do. Do you need a place to sit?"

"I think so. Do you mind sharing with me?"

She shook her head. "Not at all. I hope you know how to steer it, though, because I've never been in a canoe in my life."

"It's been a few years since I was in Boy Scouts, but I think I can manage," he said. He pointed to where Kaycee stood. "Let's go over there and pick out a boat."

Evette sat at the helm of the metal boat and did as Anthony instructed. Soon they were out on the river, paddling along at a leisurely pace. She had worried about being able to keep up with everyone, but her concerns didn't pan out.

Their group accounted for at least fifteen of the boats on the water, but several other groups had come as well. If nothing else, the first few minutes of the trip resembled a traffic jam on water.

"We can either hang back for a bit," Anthony said, "or we can speed our pace and try to maneuver around everyone else. What do you think?"

Evette's arms already felt tired so she chose the first option. "Let's hang back."

A few minutes later the logjam eased as the faster boaters got ahead of the pack and the novices moved to the rear. Evette and Anthony ended up in the middle.

"How did things go in Boston?" she asked, once they had reached a comfortable rhythm of paddling.

"It was good."

Evette waited for him to elaborate, but he seemed unwilling to say more so she changed the subject to more neutral territory. She went on and on about how things were going in the store, filled him in on local news, and even told him how her mother's garden was growing.

On the positive side her fears about the river proved unfounded. Not only was it very tame, but in some places it was almost nonexistent. The dry summer had sent the water level to record lows. In a couple of places she and Anthony had to climb out of the boat and push it through the shallow water.

Evette couldn't help but laugh as she recalled how afraid

she had been of getting swept away by the current.

After a couple of hours they paddled to the bank and joined the rest of the group for lunch. They had all been instructed to pack their own lunches with them, and Evette had kept their food in a small cooler.

While they ate, Anthony brought up his job again. "They want to hire me, but I don't think I'll go back."

"You don't?"

He shook his head. "I miss the newspaper and my family and—you."

Evette looked him in the eye. *Please let him be serious,* she prayed silently. "I missed you too."

"Evette, please tell me—were you in love with Justin when I left?"

She blew out a sigh. "No. I wasn't."

"But what about that time I saw you at the movies?"

"It was nothing. We finished inventory early and wanted to get away from work."

"You had turned me down for dinner that night, and I guess I overreacted. When you called the next day, I just—I said everything I could think of to convince myself I wouldn't be hurt if you loved him."

"And I was calling to tell you I love you," she said quietly.

"You do?"

She nodded.

"I love you too, Evette. I've been praying about this since I left. Does this mean you feel ready to have a relationship now?"

"I am now," she said, smiling. "Even though I knew I loved you when you left, I still wasn't ready. But I've been making some changes, and now I know I've reached that point where I can love Jesus and you." She looked down at the ground.

"I've already apologized to Justin, but I never got the chance to do the same with you. I did pray about a relationship with you, but I didn't give the Lord complete control over the situation. I decided to play it safe by keeping you both up in the air, in case it didn't work out with one of you."

She chuckled and continued. "My plan backfired though. By the time I admitted to Justin that I loved you, you were packing your bags and heading to Boston. Then I didn't have either one of you. I was so disappointed, and I felt so guilty."

Anthony moved and sat next to her. "Let's put all that behind us. While I was gone, I couldn't stop thinking about you. I knew I had been too hasty in making my decision to leave. I felt that I should have let you explain, but I wanted to protect myself from hearing you say you didn't want to choose me. By the time I realized I had made a mistake by leaving, I couldn't back out on my commitment to stay at the magazine for a month. So I had to wait until now. You don't know how nervous I was on the flight home."

"I was pretty nervous, too, wondering what you would say when you came back," she admitted.

The others in the group were cleaning up and heading back to their boats. Anthony and Evette followed suit and put their canoe back in the water.

Evette looked around, taking in the scenery. Today was one of the happiest days of her life. She would remember this moment for as long as she lived. Everything seemed to have fallen into place. She loved Jesus, Anthony loved Jesus, and now they loved each other. The circle was complete. Whole.

"I forgot to tell you something pretty exciting that happened," Anthony said, interrupting her thoughts.

She turned around and smiled. "What?"

"I took my golf clubs to Boston with me, and one of the

guys in the office was helping me learn."

Evette quirked an eyebrow. "How's that long game coming along?"

"Good. I can drive the ball pretty far now."

"How far?"

"Two hundred yards. Straight."

"Wow! I'm impressed. Or maybe I should be worried. After all, when you took lessons from me, you didn't do very well."

He grinned. "I guess I could say I was a little distracted by my beautiful instructor."

Evette smiled indulgently. "Well, I guess that makes up for it."

"True that. But here's the best part. We played a round yesterday since it was my last day at work. On the seventh hole, a hundred and fifty-five yard par three, I made an ace."

"You're kidding! That's awesome."

"You should have seen me jumping up and down."

"I'm impressed, Anthony. I've never done that yet. Your first hole in one."

"It made me think about you," he said, "and how much I wanted to see you and talk to you again."

"Because I was your golf teacher?"

He shook his head. "No, it was because you were always talking about how you wanted Jesus to help you feel whole. It's kind of a neat concept—whole in one. You wanted to be whole in the One who loved us so much He gave His life to save us."

"Whole in one," Evette repeated. "I like the sound of that."

"Me too," Anthony agreed.

epilogue

Six months later

Albert cleared his throat. "Brienne and I want to thank you all for being here to share our special day with us. I especially want to thank my twin brother and best friend Anthony for being there for me since day one. Literally."

Evette sat next to Anthony, who blinked back tears. She squeezed his hand, and he gave her a grateful smile.

Albert cleared his throat. "He and I have been fairly inseparable, and we've never really lived apart. So this new phase of our lives will probably take some getting used to."

He turned to face Anthony. "Thanks, Anthony, for giving me first pick when we divided the video games. That is the true test of friendship right there."

The crowd laughed loudly. "And I'm looking forward to taking my place as best man in a couple of months when you and Evette walk down the aisle." He shrugged. "I know I'm looking forward to it because, well, I like wedding cake."

Again chuckles rippled through the hall.

"I love you, and I wish you and Evette all the happiness in the world."

Anthony gently kissed Evette then stood up to embrace his brother.

She wiped away the tears that threatened to make a mess of her makeup. The Lord was indeed good.

Despite their best intentions she and Anthony hadn't found

true happiness until they were able to trust the Lord to solve matters in their lives.

And why shouldn't it be that way? A verse she had come across during her quiet time popped into her head: "Though one may be overpowered, two can defend themselves. A cord of three strands is not quickly broken."

Three strands—whole in One.

A Letter To Our Readers

Dear Reader:

In order that we might better contribute to your reading enjoyment, we would appreciate your taking a few minutes to respond to the following questions. We welcome your comments and read each form and letter we receive. When completed, please return to the following:

Rebecca Germany, Fiction Editor
Heartsong Presents
PO Box 719
Uhrichsville, Ohio 44683

1. Did you enjoy reading *Whole in One* by Aisha Ford?
   ❏ Very much! I would like to see more books by this author!
   ❏ Moderately. I would have enjoyed it more if

   _____

   _____

   _____

2. Are you a member of **Heartsong Presents**? ❏ Yes ❏ No
   If no, where did you purchase this book? _____

   _____

3. How would you rate, on a scale from 1 (poor) to 5 (superior), the cover design? _____

4. On a scale from 1 (poor) to 10 (superior), please rate the following elements.

   ____ Heroine   ____ Plot
   ____ Hero   ____ Inspirational theme
   ____ Setting   ____ Secondary characters

6. How has this book inspired your life? _____
_____
_____

7. What settings would you like to see covered in future
   Heartsong Presents books? _____
_____
_____

8. What are some inspirational themes you would like to see
   treated in future books? _____
_____
_____

9. Would you be interested in reading other **Heartsong
   Presents** titles? ❏ Yes ❏ No

10. Please check your age range:
    ❏ Under 18   ❏ 18-24
    ❏ 25-34   ❏ 35-45
    ❏ 46-55   ❏ Over 55

Name _____

Occupation _____

Address _____

City_____ State_____ Zip_____

E-mail _____

Homespun Christmas

For the good citizens of Hope, Washington, the future appears hopeless—until a small boy's crazy idea for a *Homespun Christmas* begins to turn things around.

Can the Christmas wishes of one small boy ignite the fires of optimism in the citizens of Hope once again?

Contemporary, paperback, 352 pages, 5 ³⁄₁₆" x 8"

❤ ❤ ❤ ❤ ❤ ❤ ❤ ❤ ❤ ❤ ❤ ❤ ❤ ❤

Please send me _____ copies of *Homespun Christmas*. I am enclosing $6.97 for each. (Please add $2.00 to cover postage and handling per order. OH add 6% tax.)

Send check or money order, no cash or C.O.D.s please.

Name_____

Address _____

City, State, Zip _____

To place a credit card order, call 1-800-847-8270.
Send to: Heartsong Presents Reader Service, PO Box 721, Uhrichsville, OH 44683

❤ ❤ ❤ ❤ ❤ ❤ ❤ ❤ ❤ ❤ ❤ ❤ ❤ ❤

Hearts♥ng

Any 12 Heartsong Presents titles for only $30.00*

CONTEMPORARY ROMANCE IS CHEAPER BY THE DOZEN!

Buy any assortment of twelve *Heartsong Presents* titles and save 25% off of the already discounted price of $3.25 each!

*plus $2.00 shipping and handling per order and sales tax where applicable.

HEARTSONG PRESENTS *TITLES AVAILABLE NOW:*

(If ordering from this page, please remember to include it with the order form.)

Presents

Great Inspirational Romance at a Great Price!

Heartsong Presents books are inspirational romances in contemporary and historical settings, designed to give you an enjoyable, spirit-lifting reading experience. You can choose wonderfully written titles from some of today's best authors like Hannah Alexander, Andrea Boeshaar, Yvonne Lehman, Tracie Peterson, and many others.

When ordering quantities less than twelve, above titles are $3.25 each.
Not all titles may be available at time of order.

SEND TO: **Heartsong Presents** Reader's Service
P.O. Box 721, Uhrichsville, Ohio 44683

Please send me the items checked above. I am enclosing $_____
(please add $2.00 to cover postage per order. OH add 6.25% tax. NJ add 6%.). Send check or money order, no cash or C.O.D.s, please.
To place a credit card order, call 1-800-847-8270.

NAME _____

ADDRESS _____

CITY/STATE_____ ZIP _____

HPS 10-02

Hearts♥ng Presents
Love Stories Are Rated G!

That's for godly, gratifying, and of course, great! If you love a thrilling love story but don't appreciate the sordidness of some popular paperback romances, **Heartsong Presents** is for you. In fact, **Heartsong Presents** is the *only inspirational romance book club* featuring love stories where Christian faith is the primary ingredient in a marriage relationship.

Sign up today to receive your first set of four never-before-published Christian romances. Send no money now; you will receive a bill with the first shipment. You may cancel at any time without obligation, and if you aren't completely satisfied with any selection, you may return the books for an immediate refund!

Imagine. . .four new romances every four weeks—two historical, two contemporary—with men and women like you who long to meet the one God has chosen as the love of their lives. . .all for the low price of $10.99 postpaid.

To join, simply complete the coupon below and mail to the address provided. **Heartsong Presents** romances are rated G for another reason: They'll arrive *Godspeed!*